DEDICATION

This novel is dedicated to
the children of Cambodia.

ACKNOWLEDGMENTS

For research assistance I say thank you to: the librarians at Hotchkiss Library, Sharon, Connecticut; Mei Li Lin of the Chinese Historical Society; participants of the annual Asian-American Heritage Seminar; English as a Second Language (ESL) teachers at Riverdale Country School, New York, and Flushing High School, Queens; Jean Van Rosenberg; and Dr. Betty Lee Sung.

Thanks also go to Charles Kim, Joe Kim, Michael Lin, and Christian Kim for sharing their experiences as second- and third-generation Asian Americans. Above all I am grateful to Meng Leang Kry—a Cambodian refugee now living in Sharon, Connecticut—for telling me her own story.

Then for editorial assistance three cheers for Beverly Horowitz, Diana Ajjan, Leslie Kelley, Lee Minoff, and Ginee Seo.

Even before Elizabeth Gaynor saw Brad Mulville's green pickup truck she heard its sputtering. Soon it was pulling up beside her. "Hey," Brad yelled, "you want a lift home?"

Elizabeth shook her head and kept walking.

"Come on, Liz. I'm not going to bite you. I just want to give you a ride."

As she felt the bone-chilling February wind on her face, she thought of the three-quarters of a mile she still had to walk carrying her overloaded knapsack. Although she didn't accept rides from Brad Mulville unless she was desperate, she decided this time she was desperate.

"Okay," she called back as she let her knapsack slide to the ground. "I've got a lot of stuff."

She got in, dropped her knapsack between them on the torn upholstered seat, and felt a welcome blast of hot air from the heater. Brad looked over and smiled at her.

"It's freezing out," she said.

As Brad eased the truck back into traffic Liz remembered how Brad had always loved trucks. She could picture them

as five-year-olds playing in her backyard with Brad's toy trucks. They'd lift stones with the cranes and move sand with the backhoes. She used to have fun with those trucks. She thought too of how they'd hung out together in Catholic grammar school. Everyone in the class of twenty forming one big group of friends. Now as they turned a sharp corner onto Lincoln Avenue an empty beer can rolled against her foot. Kicking it back under the seat she realized she could count on one hand the friends she still had from grammar school. I've grown apart from the others, she thought. In high school, with so many more kids to choose from, everyone's found people more like themselves to hang out with. She looked over at Brad. For her he just wasn't one of those people. Poor Brad—oversized, loud, and dumb—majoring in failure.

"So," Brad said, "your friend Ben must be pretty happy."

"Why? What happened?"

"I guess you'll be sad though. You won't be his main squeeze anymore."

"Me and Ben Lee? What are you talking about? Ben's just my science lab partner."

"But you're always with him."

Brad looked at her out of the corner of his eye. Was she blushing?

"That's because we study together," Liz explained. She shifted on the seat to avoid the broken spring. What was Brad trying to tell her about Ben? She might not be Ben's girlfriend—his "main squeeze"—but as far as she knew no one else was either. She sighed and waited for Brad to tell her what was on his mind.

"So you didn't hear?" he asked with a mischievous grin.

"Hear what?"

2

"There's a new girl in our class. A china doll for the Chinaman."

"Brad," she asked, "are you trying to tell me that there's a new girl in our class who is Asian American? Maybe Chinese?"

"Yeah, a slant-eye. A real gorgeous one. Now Ben the Chinaman can have one of his own." He winked at Liz. "And leave the pretty American girls to me." He turned on the radio and moved the dial from rock and roll to the mellow station.

No matter how cold it gets or how heavy my books are, Liz vowed, I will never again ride home with Brad Mulville. It's not worth the aggravation of trying to carry on a conversation with him.

She looked out the window and counted the number of houses that still had the dried green O of a Christmas wreath on their front doors and wondered what the new girl would be like.

Six wreaths later Brad drove the pickup into her driveway. Stepping down out of the truck Liz looked gratefully at her yellow woodframe house. She dragged her knapsack across the seat of the truck and hitched it over her shoulder. "Thanks for the ride," she said, forcing herself to smile politely.

"See you tomorrow," Brad said with a grin.

Brad's heart raced as he gunned the engine and backed out of the driveway. Liz said Ben wasn't her boyfriend. He felt happy. He was sure that Liz must know that he liked her. He was always offering her rides from school. And he practically told her he liked her by saying the thing about leaving the pretty American girls to him. Turning the radio back to the rock station he roared away, pounding the palm of his hand on the steering wheel to keep the beat of the song that played on the radio.

3

*   *   *

Elizabeth stood in the middle of her bedroom thinking of Brad. How, she asked of the four walls, how can one person be so chauvinistic, racist, and basically gross?

She sat down at her desk and took out her assignment book. It was the second month of her second term of her second year in high school and she ranked second in class standing. She didn't think class standing was such a big deal but her parents did. They thought that since she was the top student in St. Peter's Catholic grammar school, she could be the top student in high school too. She told them that class rank shouldn't be such a big deal. Her rival for class standing, the student with the highest grades in the sophomore class, had moved to Rutland at the beginning of freshman year. His name was Ben Lee.

At exactly four-fifteen, the phone rang. Before she even picked up the receiver Elizabeth knew that it was her best friend Terry. One of them always called the other as soon as she got home, just to check in. They'd been doing it ever since they were in the seventh grade, when Terry had moved from right next door out to North Avenue.

"Did you know there's a new girl in our class?" Elizabeth asked Terry.

"There is? Who is she? What's she look like?"

"I haven't seen her. Brad Mulville told me."

"Brad told you? Then he must have said what she looks like, as in, 'What a pig,' or 'Foxy.' Which is it?"

"He said she was gorgeous. That she's . . ." Elizabeth hesitated.

"That she's what?"

"Asian. He thinks Ben Lee will love it that she's Chinese or something."

"I guess it'll be nice for him," Terry commented. "I mean,

4

if you think about it, Ben would probably like to have one of his own around. Know what I mean?"

"Well, there are the two Japanese girls in the freshman class and Peter in the senior class is Korean," Elizabeth said. "Ben doesn't hang around with them or anything."

"You're right," Terry answered. "He mostly hangs out with us. I wonder why?"

"Maybe he just doesn't like them."

"Maybe," Terry agreed.

That evening, like every Wednesday, Elizabeth made spaghetti with meat sauce for dinner. Her mother, still dressed in her nurse's aide uniform, was making a salad. Moving away from the stove and standing in front of her mother, Elizabeth asked suddenly, "How do you think I look?"

Diane Gaynor looked up from the chopping board and regarded her daughter. "Fine, you look fine. Why? Did you change anything?"

Elizabeth went back to the stove. "No. It's just the same old me," she said. She shook some more oregano into the sauce. "Do you think I should change something? I mean my hair maybe? Straighten it or something?"

"I love your curly hair. Some women would give their right arm for naturally curly hair."

"Maybe I should dye it then. You know, a darker brown maybe, or black."

She's got the February blues, Diane thought. Spring will give us all a pickup. "Really, honey," she reassured her daughter. "I love your hair just the way it is."

"But you think I'm too tall, right?"

"You want to be short with straight dark hair when you're tall with light brown curly hair? How very contrary."

"You don't have to get all worked up about it, Mom." Liz stirred the sauce. "It was just a question."

5

*   *   *

The next morning needle pricks of cold stung Liz's legs as she trudged up the hill to school. I should have worn tights under my jeans and run partway to get some warmth back into my body, she thought. The school bus, filled with the lucky kids who lived more than a mile away from Ethan Allen High, rumbled around the corner behind her.

As the bus went by, Liz slowed down and looked up. Ben Lee was knocking on the window and waving. He made a little walking gesture with his index and middle fingers, which meant he was going to walk to meet her when he got off the bus. She waved back and continued her trudge up the hill, thinking about the science class they had together. She wondered if the new girl was on the school bus and if the new girl would soon be Ben's lab partner instead of her. I'd be jealous, she thought, surprised.

Minutes later Ben was walking toward her. "Hi, Liz." He had a great smile and a quiet but totally controlled air of being completely self-possessed. Liz thought this both attractive and maddening. On the one hand she liked that Ben was mysterious. On the other hand it was always hard to figure out what he was thinking. She realized suddenly that what Ben thought was beginning to mean a lot to her.

"Hi," she answered back. "How you doing?"

"Okay. Did you bring the cheesecloth for science lab?"

She reached around and patted her knapsack. "Got it."

"I've got the sponge."

"Good," she said.

He smiled again.

She smiled again.

She felt warmer now.

Ben and Liz were in the same science, math, and English

6

classes. He was in different history and phys. ed. classes and when she took art he took music. But they were in the same homeroom—which was also their room for first period English—and they sat next to one another in the third row. Terry was on the other side of Elizabeth. Joey, another of their friends, sat in front of Terry. Brad Mulville sat way in the back on the right-hand side of the room. Brad always picked the seat as far away as possible from the teacher, but on the same side as the door—for late entrances and quick exits.

Terry came up to Elizabeth and Ben in the hall outside homeroom. "Brad's right," she whispered in Liz's ear. "She's here." As the three of them walked into the room together Elizabeth saw that her own seat was occupied by their new classmate. Ben saw the new girl too. Mr. Madison was squatting next to her explaining something.

The bell rang.

Mr. Madison stood up and called out, "Good morning, everyone. Please quiet down and take your seats."

"Where should I sit, Mr. Madison?" Elizabeth asked. Everyone was quiet and staring at either Elizabeth or the new girl or darting glances back and forth between them.

"Anywhere that's free, Elizabeth," Mr. Madison answered.

"Okay," Elizabeth said, trying to sound as though she didn't care. She waited for everyone else to sit down so she could see which seats were free. Ben nodded at the new girl before taking his seat. Liz was trying not to stare, but she'd already noticed how pretty the new girl was. Pretty in a delicate way, she decided, with almond-colored skin and black straight hair. She wore a plain white blouse and a long brightly colored cotton skirt, which was surprising because it was winter. Liz thought that the new girl and

Ben looked right sitting next to one another. A matched pair.

When everyone was seated Liz walked to the one empty seat in the back of the room. Her heart sank as her body sank into the seat next to Brad Mulville.

"My lucky day," Brad whispered with a grin. "Got a pen I can borrow?"

"Class," Mr. Madison began, "as I'm sure you have noticed, we have a new student. I'd like you to welcome Dary Sing."

Everyone turned toward the new girl and smiled or gave a little wave. Some said "Hi" or "Welcome."

Dary Sing didn't say anything. Liz couldn't see her face from her seat in the back so she didn't know if Dary was smiling back at them.

"Ben," Mr. Madison continued, "I've seated Dary next to you because I'm hoping you can help her adjust. Especially with the language. She doesn't speak English very well. Actually, from what I can tell, probably not at all. Maybe you could translate for her."

The whole class was looking at Dary and Ben. He frowned and said something to her—Elizabeth guessed it was in Chinese. Dary said something to him in a whisper. Ben raised his hand.

"Yes, Ben?"

"Mr. Madison," Ben said, "I don't think she's speaking Chinese. But then I could be wrong, because I don't know much Chinese myself."

Everyone but Ben, Dary, and Mr. Madison laughed at the idea that Ben didn't speak Chinese.

"I don't see how I can help her . . ." Ben continued, "any more than anybody else."

"Bad move, slant-eyes," Brad muttered. "You could've had her following you around all day and night like a little

8

puppy dog." He turned to Elizabeth. "Don't believe that garbage about not speaking Chinese. He just doesn't want to bother."

"Shut up," Liz whispered back.

"Well, then," Mr. Madison was saying, "what shall we do here? Someone's going to have to show her around. Maybe it would be better if it were a girl."

"I think so," Ben said. "I think she's shy."

"So," Mr. Madison asked as he scanned the room, "which of you young ladies could use some service credit? I'd really appreciate it if I could get some help with this."

Should I do it? Elizabeth wondered. She didn't have any public service credits and she would need them to graduate. Terry did volunteer work at the hospital. Joey worked in the recycling program at the town dump. But, Elizabeth knew, those sorts of things would eat into her homework time. Helping Dary, she realized, was something she could do while she was in school. She thrust her hand into the air. "I'll take her around to her classes and everything," she volunteered. "I mean, if that will help."

"Thank you, Elizabeth," Mr. Madison said. "Why don't you change places with Ben then."

As Ben moved back through the aisles to sit next to Brad, and Liz moved up to sit next to Dary, she wondered, Why didn't Ben at least try to help her?

Three beeps came over the loudspeaker. Dary stared at the speaker and listened attentively as the principal, Mrs. Harmon, made announcements. But, Liz reminded herself, Dary probably doesn't understand what's being said. When announcements were over, Liz leaned over and explained, "English lesson, now."

Dary looked at her blankly. Elizabeth thought, she must be disappointed that I don't speak her language. She smiled reassuringly at Dary.

9

When Mr. Madison told them to take out their vocabulary homework Elizabeth wondered what Dary would do while the class discussed words like *deficit*, *delerium*, *deleterious*. She tried to remember how she'd learned to read and write. She quickly printed the alphabet across the top of a clean piece of paper and put it with a pencil on Dary's desk. "Al-pha-bet," she said as she made the gesture of writing. "Copy." She pointed to the letters and repeated, "Al-pha-bet."

Dary looked down at the paper, looked over at Elizabeth with a blank faraway expression, then looked back to the front of the room. She stayed like that for the rest of the period.

At the end of the period as everyone else left the room, Dary and Elizabeth stood at Mr. Madison's desk while he studied Dary's schedule. "Let's see, she has gym next period." He looked at Liz questioningly. His next class was already filing into the room.

"I have history," Liz explained. "But I'll bring her to the gym first."

"I really appreciate this, Elizabeth. Thank you."

As the two girls went into the crowded corridor, Liz tried to rush Dary along. She was already late for Ms. Simpson's history class, which meant she was late for an important quiz.

"Gym," she explained to Dary as they went toward the gym. "That's like exercise. You play games." She made a gesture like throwing a ball into a basket.

"Play?" Dary said.

"Yes." Liz grinned. "Play."

Dary smiled back. "Play," she repeated.

Liz pointed to the sign on the big metal doors leading into the gym. "G-Y-M," she said. "Gym."

Dary repeated, "Gym."

Liz introduced Dary to the gym teacher—Mr. Martin. Since Dary didn't have shorts and shoes for gym, she'd be spending the period watching.

As Liz rushed into history class Ms. Simpson glared at her over the rim of her glasses. "Ms. Gaynor, thank you for joining us."

Elizabeth didn't waste time trying to explain, but went right to her desk where the mimeographed sheet of questions was staring up at her. She looked up, catching Terry's eye. "It's murder," Terry mouthed.

Forty minutes later as she and Terry were leaving the room, Liz said, "Well, there was no way I aced that one. I didn't even have time to read over what I wrote for the essay question."

"One B isn't going to kill you." Terry leaned sideways and asked, "So, what's she like?"

"Who?"

"Dary what's-her-name?"

"I don't know. I mean, she can't speak English, Terry. I think she's sort of scared. And confused. So far she knows one word—*play*—oh, yeah, and *gym*."

"That's useful," Terry said, "if she meets a guy named Jim."

Sometimes Elizabeth had lunch with Ben, especially if there was homework for a science lab that they were working on together. But by the time she got to the cafeteria and in line with Dary, Ben was already sitting with Joey and some of the other guys. She saw that Terry had a tray of food and was saving a place for her at a small corner table.

"Hot lunch," Liz told Dary as she pointed to a tray of

11

bright yellow macaroni and cheese and another tray of dull green cooked string beans. "You want some?"

Dary shook her head no.

She's got to eat something, Elizabeth thought, and put a ham and cheese sandwich on Dary's tray. But when Terry and Elizabeth ate their lunch Dary just sat there. Liz pointed to the carton of milk she'd picked up for her. "Drink the milk."

She opened Dary's carton, put in the straw, and then took a sip of her own milk. "Drink."

Finally Dary bent over and sucked on the straw. She made such a disgusted expression that Liz thought she would spit it out, but finally she swallowed.

A few minutes later, when they were leaving the cafeteria, Dary patted her stomach.

"If she's hungry," Terry asked, "why didn't she eat?"

Before Liz could ponder this mystery Dary was throwing up in the big gray garbage bin at the door of the cafeteria. Liz had to bring Dary to the nurse in the infirmary, which made her late for science lab. She hoped the rest of the week would be easier for both of them.

During lab Ben was in one of his intense academic moods and they only talked about their experiment. She wanted to ask him why he didn't help Dary. Why he didn't ask how she was doing. Was Brad right about Ben understanding Dary's language, but not wanting to be bothered with translating for her? Did he just not care—or did he really have a crush on Dary and was being super careful not to let anyone know?

A few minutes later, when Liz handed Ben back his lab book, their hands touched. She pictured the two of them holding hands, and her heart beat faster. She wondered what it would be like to go on a date with Ben Lee.

* * *

"Want to come to my house?" Terry asked Liz at the end of the day. "You can get on the bus with the rest of us. My mother will bring you home when she gets out of work. You can see the outfit I got for the Valentine's Day dance."

They passed the school infirmary, where the nurse was standing in the doorway. "Elizabeth," she called out. "Could I see you for a minute?"

The girls walked over to her.

"Mrs. Harmon would like you to go to her office, Elizabeth. It's about Dary Sing."

"That's your answer," Liz told Terry. "I can't go with you."

The nurse walked along the corridor with her. "What did Dary have for lunch?" she asked.

"She didn't eat anything. I got her a sandwich but she wouldn't eat it. And she hated the milk. Does she just like chop suey and rice and stuff like that?"

"Did she drink any of the milk?"

"Just a sip. I mean she really hated it. You'd think it was poison or something."

"To her it probably was," the nurse explained. "She may be lactose intolerant."

"Does that mean she's allergic to anything with milk in it?" Liz asked.

"Precisely."

"What a bummer," Liz concluded. She knocked on the principal's door and went in. Mrs. Harmon was at her desk. Dary and a woman were sitting in straight-backed chairs in front of the desk.

Mrs. Harmon introduced Elizabeth to the woman—Mrs. Dahm—whom Liz recognized as a waitress at Sewards. Mrs. Dahm stood and bowed toward her. "Thank you. Thank you," Mrs. Dahm said as she tipped toward Liz again. "Good friend to help Dary. Very, very nice girl."

Liz smiled and said, "You're welcome." She wondered if the woman was Dary's mother. But then she figured that she wasn't because Dary and Mrs. Dahm had different last names and the Dahm family had been living in Rutland for at least two years. Dary was new to town.

"Mrs. Dahm is Dary's aunt," Mrs. Harmon explained. "And I agree with her. We're all grateful to you, Elizabeth, for helping Dary."

"She got sick," Liz reminded everyone. "The nurse said she's probably allergic to milk."

"Do you understand?" Mrs. Harmon asked Mrs. Dahm.

"Yes, yes," she answered. "No milk. Bad for Cambodian." She rubbed her stomach the way Dary did before she threw up.

"Does Dary speak Chinese?" Liz asked.

"Khmer," Mrs. Dahm answered. "Only Khmer. Little English. I teach. Camp teach."

What camp? Liz wondered. She told them, "Dary doesn't understand me."

Mrs. Dahm asked Dary something in Khmer. Dary answered. Mrs. Dahm told Liz, "She understand you her friend. You help her learn English. Very important. To learn. To study. Very important."

Dary must be very tired, Liz thought, with everything being so new and confusing and throwing up on top of it all.

For the rest of the meeting Mrs. Harmon and Mr. Madison explained Dary's new schedule to Elizabeth. They were going to get an English teacher to work privately with Dary for one period a day. The rest of the day Dary was to follow Liz around to her classes, learning whatever she could, while she adjusted to her new language, her new country, and her new school.

* * *

"I don't know how it happened," Liz told Terry over the phone an hour later. "I mean, I was just going to help her get to her classes. I didn't think they'd give her to me full-time, for lunch and everything. I already hate it. It'll be like babysitting all day."

"I guess Ben knew what he was doing."

"What do you mean?"

"I mean by not getting involved."

Before closing the refrigerator door Elizabeth's mother asked her, "Honey, do you want some milk?"

"Uh, no. No milk." She remembered the milky mess that Dary heaved up. "I'll have apple juice."

On Thursday nights Liz's father kept his shoe store open until nine o'clock, so Liz and her mother ate dinner alone. That night they were having takeout Chinese that Diane picked up on her way home from the hospital.

"So, how was your day?" she asked her daughter as she handed her the glass of juice and sat down in front of her.

"Okay." Liz twirled the sesame noodles around the chopsticks and wondered if Ben's father made them. Or his mother. As the noodles slid down her throat she realized that in all the times she'd gone to Lee's Chinese she'd never seen Ben there.

"Your day was just okay?" Diane asked. "Is school that boring?"

"It wasn't boring. Not at all. Guess what? I finally got a service credit assignment."

"Really. Where is it? If it's at the hospital, I could talk to the director of volunteer services about getting you something interesting to do that wouldn't take too much time from your schoolwork—maybe in the computer room."

"Actually it's right in school," Elizabeth said. As they ate chicken and snow peas with brown rice, Liz told her mother about Dary, explaining how she'd be responsible for Dary almost the whole school day.

"The important thing, honey, is that you don't let this interfere with your schoolwork. You're a student, not a teacher. You and that young Chinese boy are neck and neck for first place. You know how proud we'd be if you graduated valedictorian of your class. If you work hard your father and I have no doubts you can get a scholarship to the University of Vermont. You can do it if you put your schoolwork first."

"Mom," Liz interrupted, "maybe I should just go to my room and study right now."

Diane smiled. "I'm sorry. End of lecture. Eat up. Let's talk about that dance you're going to Saturday night."

By the time they'd thrown away the food cartons and washed the chopsticks Liz had negotiated a midnight curfew for the night of the dance.

In the cafeteria line on Friday the only thing Dary took to eat was an orange. This is ridiculous, Liz thought. Isn't there anything here she'll eat?

As Terry and Elizabeth ate the cafeteria's English muffin version of pizza they talked about what they were going to wear to the Valentine's Day dance. Liz felt guilty when she saw that Dary—not understanding what they were talking about—was staring off into space again.

Liz leaned over and showed her the picture that Terry had sketched of her new outfit. Liz wrote "d-r-e-s-s" and

18

said it slowly. Dary repeated, "Dress." Then Liz drew a girl in the dress and labeled the body parts—"h-e-a-d," "a-r-m," "l-e-g"—saying the words as she wrote them.

Now Terry was looking off into space. She got up and told Liz, "I'll be right back. I've got to talk to Joey about something." Liz watched Terry going over to the table where their friends were having a great old time. I shouldn't do service credit during lunch hour, Liz decided. It's practically the only time I have with my friends. Ben was telling a story that made everyone laugh. A cute, brainy guy who can make you laugh, Liz thought. That's Ben.

She was wondering how she could get rid of Dary during her lunch periods when she noticed that Dary was writing on the labeled drawing, painstakingly copying letter by letter the words Liz had written, silently trying to mouth the words as she wrote them. Liz pointed to the word and said, "Arm." Dary repeated it. Liz added facial features to the drawing and labeled them, "e-y-e-s," "n-o-s-e," "m-o-u-t-h." Then they practiced those.

Twenty minutes later, when the bell rang for the next class, Terry came back to their table and bent over to whisper in Liz's ear, "I hope you're not going to invite Dary to the dance. It would be really tough to have her hanging around. Don't you think?"

"Yeah," Liz agreed as she imagined the dance with a-r-m-s and l-e-g-s moving and shaking to the rock and roll music. "That would definitely be an overload of culture shock."

She pulled the page they'd been working on out of Terry's notebook and handed it to Dary. "For you," she said. "Homework."

"Thank you," Dary said as she bowed to Liz just the way Mrs. Dahm had. "Thank you."

As Liz walked down the hill toward home after school

she let out a deep sigh of relief. A freezing wind gusted out of the steel gray sky, but she felt lighthearted and happy. There was a dance on Saturday and she knew she'd have a great time with her friends. And she didn't have to worry about Dary Sing until Monday morning.

"You look terrific, honey," Diane Gaynor said as she watched Liz come down the stairs Saturday night. "Long legs, curly brown hair, and all."

"You think so?" Liz said, even though she knew that she looked great in a red silk blouse and short, straight black skirt.

Diane went up two steps so she could see the top of Liz's head. She adjusted the red and black barrettes that held her daughter's curls off her face. "Your barrettes are exactly the same shade of red as your lipstick," she said. "You look great. Absolutely. You'll be breaking every guy's heart at that Valentine's Day dance."

"Breaking hearts? That's a pretty old-fashioned idea, Mom. I just want to have a good time."

"Do you mean to say there isn't one special boy in that school you'd like to notice you tonight? No one who might have sent you this?" She held out a card. "I can't believe you didn't check the mailbox on Valentine's Day."

"Probably a friendship card from Terry," Liz said as she took the envelope. "Or you. Very tricky, Mom." But the handwriting on the card wasn't her mother's or Terry's. The address was printed, the way a little kid would write or someone trying to disguise their handwriting.

"Aren't you going to open it and end the mystery?" Diane asked.

"Sure. Why not?"

Liz unsealed the envelope and pulled out a card. It was

an old-fashioned card, with a large red heart in the middle surrounded by raised roses. She opened it. Under a short verse she saw: "Love, B."

"So?" her mother asked.

"Private," Liz said, a blush of embarrassment adding yet another red highlight to her Valentine's Day outfit. She closed the card and stuffed it back into the envelope. She turned around and started back up the stairs. "I forgot my, ah, perfume. Be right back."

Well, Diane thought with a pleased little smile, a boyfriend. I guess it's about time. She thought of all Liz's school friends, picturing them like photos in a yearbook. It's probably that nice Joey Gregorio, she concluded.

Liz sat on the edge of her bed and opened the card again. It simply asked, "Will you be my Valentine?" Liz studied the "Love, B." and thought, *Ben.*

Half an hour later Liz, Terry, and Joey walked into the gym together. The seniors had decorated it with red and black streamers. Strobe lights whirled and flashed their mysterious pulsating blinks of cool white light. The rock band, dressed in red and black, was warming up. "You should be on the stage," Terry told Liz. "You'd fit right in."

"Do you think I look silly?"

"I do," Joey teased. "I think you both look silly." He laughed nervously because he was absolutely knocked out by how beautiful Terry looked in a hot pink dress. Or was it the way she fixed her hair off her face like that? Or something about her complexion? When he snuck another glance at Terry she was looking at him as though she was thinking that he was pretty great too.

Meanwhile Liz was looking around the gym, wondering

if "B" was there. If he'd even come. Even though Ben was popular, he was the type who came to parties and mostly hung out with the guys and then left early. Terry said he went home early because his parents were very strict and expected him to study.

"Where's your new sidekick?" Joey asked Liz, to cover his embarrassment at getting caught staring at Terry.

"Sidekick?"

"The new girl. Mary." He ran his fingers through his tightly cropped black hair. "I thought I'd ask her to dance. You know, so she doesn't feel left out or anything."

"Dary," Liz corrected. "Her name's Dary. I don't think she's coming." She felt a pang of guilt for not having invited her.

Terry felt incredible relief that Dary wasn't there. "It'd probably be too much culture shock for her," Terry explained to Joey. He nodded in agreement.

A strong arm went around Liz's waist and a big hand rubbed the silk on her back. "Hey, Liz," Brad whispered. "You look great."

She shrugged him off with a quick "Thanks" and turned away from him to face Terry. Terry took the hint and got into a conversation with her about the decorations. All the while Liz prayed that Brad wouldn't ask her to dance.

After talking to Joey for a few seconds, Brad tapped Liz on the shoulder. "Catch you later," he said and he went over to his upperclassmen buddies.

"Brad's beginning to get on my nerves," Liz told Terry.

"Hey," Joey said, "there's Ben." He waved and called out, "Ben. Over here."

Liz had plenty of time to study Ben as he moved toward them across the big open space of the dance floor. She

22

decided he was definitely the best-dressed guy at the dance. In his navy blue blazer, light blue shirt, striped tie, and khakis he looked just perfect. So many kids greeted him as he passed that she realized again how popular Ben was.

She watched Ben and Brad pass one another. Brad gave Ben a light jab on the arm and said something that sent a flash of anger over Ben's face. Liz glanced at Terry and Joey to see whether they'd noticed, but they were too busy looking at one another.

When Ben reached them Joey told him, "I could've given you a ride."

"No problem," Ben said. "But maybe I'll take a lift home." He looked around at Terry and Liz. "Hi."

The band pulled it together and started their first number. Terry was moving to the beat and snapping her fingers without really dancing. The lead guitarist spoke into the mike above the noise of his band, "All right. Let's go. Everyone on the floor. It's time to get down and *boogie.*"

As Terry's little movements let loose into real dancing Joey pulled her out on the floor. Ben and Liz watched them dance.

"Terry's a great dancer," Liz shouted above the music.

Joey and Terry danced back over to them. "Let's go, you guys," Joey said as he pulled Liz out onto the floor.

"Come on, Ben," Terry shouted.

The four of them started dancing together. Soon, Liz realized, it was Ben dancing with her and Terry dancing with Joey. And Ben was a terrific dancer. He had a loose, easy foot movement and danced with his whole body, not with a stiff upper body like some guys.

It was fun to move with him. They went for three songs

23

in a row. Then the tempo changed and the melody turned into a romantic song. Terry and Joey went toward the sidelines for a soda with some other kids from their class. "Coming?" Terry called. But Liz didn't follow her. Instead she moved toward Ben. They had danced for three songs without touching. She wanted to dance close. They looked into each other's eyes as she moved still closer. He put an arm around her waist. She held his hand. They turned and moved and were closer than they'd ever been. Neither of them spoke. Liz closed her eyes.

She was thinking about how much she enjoyed being with him, enjoyed this comfortable, close, slow-moving feeling when Ben let go of her. She opened her eyes and saw Brad. "Okay, Elizabeth," he told her. "You can dance with me now."

Before Elizabeth could answer, Ben said, "Leave us alone."

"Look, slant-eyes, why don't you stick to your own kind," Brad bit out. "You got a new pretty one in our class now, so just leave the American girls to us."

Ben dropped his arm from around Liz's waist. He didn't say anything more to Brad, just stared at him for a moment, turned, and walked off the floor.

Liz turned to follow Ben, to tell him not to pay any attention to Brad. But Brad held her by the wrist. "I was just breaking in," he said. "I wanted to dance with you."

"Well I don't want to dance with you," she said. "So get your hands off me."

As she moved quickly away from him she heard Brad ask whoever was close by, "What's wrong with her?"

Liz found Terry and Joey at the snack table. "Where's Ben?" Terry asked.

"I don't know," Liz answered as she looked around the

24

gym. "Maybe he went to the men's room." She wanted to find Ben. She'd tell him about Brad. How since they were little kids he'd sometimes say things that hurt people's feelings, always pushing and shoving. But five minutes later Ben still wasn't in the gym.

"Ben probably went home to study," Terry joked.

"Why do you always say that?" Liz snapped. "He doesn't study any more than I do. Brad cut in when we were dancing and he made some stupid racist remark to Ben. He must have left because he was hurt or mad or something."

"Well Brad can be pretty stupid and I'm not surprised he's a racist," Terry said. "But nobody takes Brad seriously. Doesn't Ben know that?"

"What Brad said was awful. And he cut in like he owned me."

"You're probably more upset about it than Ben," Terry said. "So what if Brad cut in? It's not like Ben's your boyfriend." She moved back on the dance floor with Joey.

The rest of the evening wasn't much fun for Liz. When she finally left with Terry and Joey they passed Brad and his pals in the parking lot. Brad was cursing because he had a flat tire on his pickup. He kicked the tire. "I tell you, that chink spiked my tire. Sneaky yellow bastard. He'll pay for this."

"Brad *is* disgusting," Terry admitted.

"I wouldn't blame Ben if he did blow the tire," Joey mumbled as they got into his father's station wagon.

Terry said, "Me either."

Liz didn't say anything.

Hours after she'd gone to bed Elizabeth still wasn't asleep. First she worried about Brad threatening Ben. Then she remembered how it felt to dance close to Ben. When she

25

was in eighth grade she thought she was dying of love for Tim Prescott. They danced close at parties, snuck kisses, talked on the phone for hours, and that summer before high school they hung around with one another at the town pool. Then it fizzled out. She tried to remember if her feelings for Tim were like her feelings for Ben and she knew there was no comparison. What she felt for Ben wasn't just puppy love.

What will happen next between Ben and me? she wondered. Will he call and ask for a date? Maybe he'll slip me another note as we leave science lab, signed "Love, B."

It was three in the morning when she got up, turned on her desk lamp, and sat down to write a note to Ben Lee. After a lot of thought and many false starts she wrote:

> Dear B.
>
> I'm sorry about what happened at the dance with Brad and I understand why you did that to his truck. But, Ben, don't make trouble with Brad. He's not worth it.
>
> I'm glad we danced. I had a good time. I'm sorry that you left early. After you left, the dance wasn't much fun.
>
> Love, E.

As she reread the note she stopped on the name "Brad." B-R-A-D. Brad, she realized, begins with *B* too. Images flashed through her mind like scenes in a movie. Brad always offering her a ride home from school. Brad being so happy when she sat next to him in the back of the room. Brad putting his arm around her when she first came to the dance. Brad breaking in when she was dancing with Ben, saying, "I wanted to dance with you."

26

Liz's throat tightened as she wondered, what if Brad sent me the Valentine's Day card instead of Ben?

She remembered Terry and Joey pulling her and Ben onto the dance floor. It wasn't as if Ben asked her to dance. She saw herself moving toward him, inviting him with her eyes and body to dance close. Maybe, she thought, Ben didn't want to dance with me at all.

She tore up the note she'd written to Ben Lee and got back into bed feeling more confused and embarrassed than in love.

"Liz, Liz. Wake up." It was Terry's voice.

Liz rolled over and opened her eyes. Terry was sitting on the edge of the bed. "I've been waiting forever for you to wake up."

"I'm awake. What time is it?"

"Ten o'clock. You won't believe what's happening."

Liz sat up, rubbed her eyes, and asked, "What's going on?"

"It's Joey and me. I mean, all of a sudden it's like we're more than just friends."

"That's great."

Terry knelt on the bed. "Now we have to find someone for you. There's no one in our class. So maybe a junior. Joey and I are already talking about who to set you up with. Just think: double-dating. We'll have so much fun."

Liz looked at Terry and rubbed her eyes again. What about Ben? Why doesn't Terry think of Ben and me double-dating with her and Joey? Aren't the four of us always together anyway? Doesn't she think Ben counts as a real guy? Does she dismiss him just because he's Asian?

"Don't you think so?" Terry asked.

"What? Don't I think so, what?"

"Joey and me. That we're like the greatest together? I mean you're not jealous or anything?" Terry's eyes were filling up with tears as they anxiously searched Elizabeth's face. "You look so sad. Oh, Liz, you don't have a crush on Joey too?"

Elizabeth laughed. "Me and Joey? No. I think you and Joey are great together. Haven't I always said that?"

Terry gave Elizabeth a hug. "I'm so glad you're happy for me."

Elizabeth was halfway to school on Monday morning when it started to snow. Dary was among the other under-a-mile hikers, only she'd stopped walking. As other kids moved around her Dary was looking straight up at the tumbling snowflakes that landed like polka dots on her navy blue coat.

Walking toward Dary, Liz realized that Dary had never seen snow before. Liz hoped she wasn't frightened by it. But Dary was smiling. When she saw Elizabeth she gleefully said, "Snow."

Liz looked up at the big bouncy flakes that tumbled down through the leaden gray sky and melted on her face. "Pretty snow," she said.

"Bea-oo-ti-ful," Dary added.

The school bus went by them, wheels squeaking on fresh snow. Liz watched it pass, but Ben didn't wave.

The first people Liz noticed when she walked into the classroom were Ben and Joey in the back talking and laughing. She thought, if I were Ben and I had punctured one of Brad Mulville's tires I wouldn't be laughing; I'd be scared and nervous about seeing Brad in school—particularly if I sat right next to him. It occurred to her for the first time

that Ben might not have spiked the tire and that he might not even realize that Brad thought he did.

She went to the back of the room and leaned against the edge of Ben's desk. "Did you tell him?" she asked Joey.

"What?" both boys asked.

Elizabeth looked at Ben. "Brad thinks you spiked the tire on his pickup Saturday. When you left the dance."

"Why would I do that?" Ben asked.

"Because of the way he talked to you I guess." Elizabeth swallowed a nervous cough, then added, "When we were dancing."

"What'd he say to you?" Joey asked Ben.

"It was no big deal," Ben said. "I don't pay any attention to that kind of talk. It's ignorant prejudice. I don't have time for it."

If it really didn't bother him, Liz thought, he wouldn't have gone home early.

The bell rang. Mr. Madison was calling out, "To your places, class," when Brad came into the room yelling, "I'm not late. I'm here." He took four big strides up the aisle and straddled his seat without even taking off his coat.

"Be careful," Elizabeth mouthed to Ben while sidling past him to go back to her own seat. She ignored Brad.

Maybe I shouldn't have mentioned the tire business to Ben, Liz thought as she sat down and opened her notebook. Maybe Brad realizes that spiking tires isn't the sort of thing Ben Lee would do.

But in science lab that afternoon Ben handed her a slip of paper. It read: "One truck tire, $96.00. You better git me this mony by Fri.!" Instead of a signature there was a large printed "B." The printing on the bill matched the printing on the envelope of the Valentine's Day card. Her heart turned over, her stomach sank. The note was absolute proof that Brad, not Ben, had sent her the Valentine.

"What are you going to do?" she whispered.

Ben shrugged his shoulders.

"Could I have everyone's attention?" the science teacher, Mr. Reeves, called out. "Including you two whiz kids over there."

Mr. Reeves smiled at Liz and Ben but he did mean business, so they couldn't talk for the rest of the class, and when the bell rang Liz had to rush to meet Dary at the gym and bring her to art class.

"This will be fun," Liz told Dary as they walked together through the room of easels. "It's like play." At least in this class, Liz thought, Dary won't have to worry so much about words. She introduced Dary to the art teacher, Max Thomas. Max was the only teacher that the students called by his first name, probably because he was not a regular teacher, but a local artist who taught the painting class. Max set Dary up with an easel and canvas. As Liz squeezed out some of the acrylic paints for her she wondered if Dary had ever painted before, if she understood they'd be copying the still-life of flowers and fruit that Max had set up on a stool in the middle of the room.

Handing Dary a long-handled bristle brush, she said, "This is a brush."

Dary held the brush up between their faces. "Brush. What letter?" While everyone else started their painting, Elizabeth wrote out words for Dary on a clean page in her notebook—"canvas," "brush," "paint," "charcoal."

Tom Greene, who stood next to Liz in the class, smiled to himself as he sketched. When he'd outlined the apple on his canvas he pointed to it and told Dary, "Apple." She looked at Liz expectantly, a look that said, "What letters?"

Liz wrote "A-P-P-L-E" under the list of other words.

Max came over to them. "Is this still an art class?" he asked with a wry grin. "Or am I in the wrong room?"

32

"Looks more like an English class, doesn't it?" Liz commented.

He said to Dary, "Liz paints." He made the gestures of painting. "Dary paints." He smiled at her. "No words needed."

Dary filled a brush with paint. She did a quick painting of an apple and labeled it in carefully painted letters, "A-P-P-L-E." After she'd painted the vase she looked at Liz. Liz said, "Vase" and spelled "V-A-S-E." Dary copied the letters in bright blue paint. That's how the class went, with Dary learning how to say and write everything she painted. She'd quickly paint, then painstakingly write the word with her brush. By the time the bell rang she'd managed to fit in "window," "desk," "door," and "wall," on her canvas. Words, words, words. Liz had barely gotten started on her own still-life.

After school Liz hung around the corridor pretending to look for something in the back of her locker so Ben wouldn't know that she was waiting for him.

"Hi," Ben said as he opened his own locker. "How was art class?"

She was about to tell him how cute and intense Dary was and how she'd filled her canvas with words, but decided not to. "It was okay. What are you going to do about Brad?"

"I don't know yet."

"Aren't you scared? He's huge. He also has this wicked temper. Before you came here, in seventh grade, he—"

"It's all right, Elizabeth, you don't have to worry. I'll think of something. I can handle it."

"Aren't you even a little scared?" she asked just as three seniors in all their hockey gear came down the hall. They were talking and not about to break up their group to fit by

33

Liz and Ben. Liz moved closer to Ben to get out of the way. After the seniors had passed, Ben put his arm around her shoulder and pulled her even closer. They looked into each other's eyes. For once she knew exactly what Ben Lee was thinking. I want to stay like this, she thought.

"Scared of Brad?" Ben said. "No way. Maybe just a little apprehensive. The thing is, I have something Brad doesn't have."

"What's that?" Liz asked as they separated.

"Smarts." He looked at his watch. "I better hurry. The bus."

After he'd left, Liz packed up her things. As she headed home she couldn't help wondering, does Ben think he's smarter than everyone in the school, including me? Is he?

The school bus was pulling away from the building as she came out the front doors into the cold. The fresh snow was only an inch deep, but the street was icy.

"E-li-a-bet," a voice called behind her. Liz turned. Dary. "Bery cold," Dary observed. Liz remembered that the Dahm family lived in an apartment near downtown, which was only a few blocks from her own street. As the two girls headed down the slippery hill together Liz wondered if Dary would now expect to walk with her every day. Will she wait at her corner each morning until she sees me? Will another hour out of my day be devoted to teaching Dary English?

She watched Dary out of the corner of her eye. Dary was so cold her teeth were chattering.

Halfway down the hill a honking horn and a crunching tire on the salted asphalt announced Brad Mulville in his pickup truck. He called through the open window, "Hey, you girls look cold. Wanna ride?"

For half a second Liz considered his offer. Dary looked so cold and they weren't even halfway home. But when she

turned to tell Dary, she saw Dary was backing away. There was a frightened look in her eyes, a tenseness in her body that Liz noticed even through the winter clothing.

Liz moved toward her, asking, "What's wrong?"

Dary backed away farther.

Brad yelled, "Hey come on. Tell her I don't bite."

"No," Dary whispered to Liz through chattering teeth. "No go."

"It's okay," Liz reassured her. "We'll walk."

"You go ahead," Liz yelled to Brad. She tried to sound friendly so that Dary wouldn't become more upset. "She's nervous with strangers."

Brad looked vaguely hurt and disappointed. "Hey man, these foreigners are driving me crazy. I'm just trying to be nice. What about you, Liz?"

"I'll walk with Dary. Thanks anyway."

As Brad roared away in his truck he jacked up the volume on the radio's rock and roll station. Man, he thought, these foreigners are nothing but trouble for me.

"Let's go," Liz told Dary. "It's cold standing still." As they continued walking Liz wanted to distract Dary from whatever was freaking her out. She started teaching Dary new words. By the time they'd reached her apartment Dary knew *house, tree, branch, ice, gray,* and *sky.* Pointing, saying, and then spelling.

Fifteen minutes later Liz dumped her books and notebooks on her desk. Before tackling her homework she looked around her room. *Window, door, picture.* She saw them identified with Dary's brightly painted words.

She picked up the phone and punched the numbers for her father's shoe store. When he answered she asked, "You know those little pads you have in your office? The ones you stick to things and then take off?"

"Post-its?" he guessed.

"Yeah. Those things. Do you have an extra pack that you could bring home for me?"

"I'm all out," he told her. "But I'll pick some up at the pharmacy on the way home. Marian Parenti stocks them."

"You don't have to do that, Dad. I can get them myself. Maybe tomorrow."

"I'd be glad to do it, honey. Nothing is too much trouble if it's for your education."

"Could you get me three then—in different colors?" She didn't tell her father that the labels weren't for her education but were for Dary's.

After dinner Liz was back at her desk. Her mind wandered to how she and Ben had sort of embraced at the locker, and how good it felt. The phone rang. "Ben?" The only times Ben and I have talked on the phone, Liz thought when she heard his voice on the other end, were the few times he's called me about homework. "Did you do the algebra?" she asked.

"Yeah. It was easy."

It's not the homework, she thought as she took the phone over to her bed and stretched out. Maybe we're turning into a boy and girl who talk on the phone. She loved the idea. But what would they talk about? "Pretty cold out," she said.

"Yeah. And it's getting colder. Ten below tomorrow with a windchill factor of thirty below. Fahrenheit, of course."

"Have you figured out what you're going to do about Brad?" Liz asked. "The bill and everything . . ."

"That's what I called about. Brad thinks I gave him a flat tire and I didn't. I have to find out how his tire got flat. Will you tell me something more about him? It might help me figure this out."

Elizabeth sat up on the bed and leaned back against the headboard. "Brad's always had a hot temper, but lately

36

he's been acting like such a dumb jerk. He's never been good at schoolwork. Every year the teachers threaten to hold him back but because he's so big the school finds an excuse to push him right along to the next grade."

"Where does he live?"

"Spear Street. It's not like he's one of these abused kids you feel sorry for. My parents know his parents. They're nice people. I played with Brad a lot when we were little so I've known him practically forever. And in grammar school he was part of the group that I hung out with. You know, like with Terry and Joey."

"You were friends with Brad?"

"Well, yes. It was a small school. Everyone in our grade got along real well. If you had a birthday party you invited everyone."

"I never would have thought that."

"Thought what?"

"That you'd be friends with someone like Brad."

"It's no big deal," Liz said as she put a pillow behind her head and wondered if Ben was only friends with people who are really smart. "Brad's gotten worse since we came to high school," she explained. "But he's never been as mean and stupid as he's been about you."

"Does he have a job after school?"

"He works at Hadley's Hardware. That's why he's got the truck. It's Mr. Hadley's truck. He lets Brad drive it because of deliveries and everything."

"And Hadley has a lumberyard too."

"Yeah."

"Great."

"Why great?"

"Brad probably ran over a nail at work and had a slow leak."

"I bet that is what happened. But how are you going to prove it if you don't have the old tire?"

37

"That's what I have to work on next," Ben explained. Liz knew that excitement and pleasure were dancing in his eyes. Ben loved to solve problems.

They talked some more, not about anything special. It just felt special because it was Ben. "Well," Liz finally said, "see you in school tomorrow."

"Tomorrow. See you then."

After Liz hung up she hugged herself and bounced on the bed. Ben and me, she thought, it feels so right. I love the way he looks, the way he talks, the way he thinks. I love Ben.

She got up, put her favorite tape in the tape deck, and danced around the room, first alone, then with her reflection in the full-length mirror on the closet door. While the song continued, she stopped abruptly and studied her reflection. She leaned forward and stared at her face. She put her fingers to her temples and stretched the skin, feeling the pull across the eyelids. That's all it is, she decided, a different shape to the eye. A flatter face. Skin that's yellowish instead of pinkish or brownish. People have all sorts of different features. And colors. So what's the big deal? Who cares if an Italian/Irish American girl is falling in love with a Chinese American guy?

FOUR

In the morning, before leaving for school, Liz looked up "Dahm" in the phone book and dialed Dary's aunt.

"This is Elizabeth Gaynor," she explained. "The girl from school who's helping Dary."

"Hello. Thank you for being a good friend to Dary."

"Dary is working real hard," Liz said. "To learn English."

"Work hard," Mrs. Dahm repeated. "You very good teacher. Many new words every day."

"I pass your apartment on the way to school," Liz told her. "I can walk to school with Dary." She'd decided not to mention to Mrs. Dahm how anxious Dary seemed around Brad. "If we walk together it will give us extra time to practice English."

"Very nice girl," Mrs. Dahm said. "Thank you very much."

Liz glanced at her watch. "So I'll be there in about fifteen minutes." Then, noticing the little pile of yellow, pink, and blue Post-its on her desk, she added, "Maybe Dary can come to my house on Sunday afternoon and I can help her some more."

"No go to other house. Stay in own house. I tell Dary: 'Stay home and study. No time to play.' "

"But we'll study," Liz explained. "That's why I want to have her come here. To help her more with learning English."

"Maybe, to study, is okay."

As they were cleaning up at the end of science lab Ben told Liz, "I'm going to Hadley's Lumberyard after school. To check out that tire business."

"I'll go with you."

He handed her a clean beaker to dry. "You don't have to. It's my problem with Brad. I can handle it."

"I was there when this whole thing started," she said. Ben looked at her quizzically. "I mean, Brad thinks you spiked his tire because you got angry about what he said to you when we were dancing."

"That's right. It's all your fault," he kidded.

"Right. So let me help."

"Okay. Meet me at the lockers after last period." He smiled. Liz wondered, is he remembering what I'm remembering—how we held each other the last time we were at the lockers together?

An hour later, when they were getting their jackets and packing their books, Liz told Ben that she'd promised to walk home with Dary. Dary was probably waiting for her at the main entrance that very minute. "It's no big deal," Liz explained. "It's on our way to Hadley's."

Ben sounded annoyed when he asked, "You walk her back and forth to school? Doesn't she know the way? It's pretty simple."

Liz told him what happened with Brad and the truck and how frightened Dary was. "Brad's beginning to give me the creeps too," Liz continued. "He sent me a Valentine's Day card. I guess that's why he cut in on us at the dance."

"He wants to go out with you? How could he imagine that a girl like you could be interested in him?"

"I guess because we all hung out together in grammar school."

"It's about time someone taught Brad a lesson," Ben said.

They met Dary at the school entrance and headed down the street. A strained silence took the place of their conversation moments before. Ben clammed up completely, his face blank, while Dary trudged quietly alongside. Neither of them spoke, even to Liz, who walked between them, trying to think of a way to get them all talking. What was the matter with Ben anyway? she asked herself. He was never this unfriendly with anyone. Finally she told Ben, "Dary is learning English very quickly. Maybe you know her aunt, Mrs. Dahm—she works at Sewards."

"Oh."

A group of kids, walking in the other direction, passed by them. Helen, Liz's partner from gym class, gave her a peculiar look when she said hi. Liz wondered if that was because she was one Caucasian girl with two Asians. Well, what was so weird about that? She turned her attention to Dary. Feeling the arm of her own coat, she said, "Coat."

"Coat," Dary repeated in a whisper.

Liz pointed to the sky. "Sky." She could barely hear Dary repeat, "Sky."

Dary had been quiet and seemed sort of depressed all day. Liz wondered if she'd made a mistake inviting Dary to her house on the weekend. At that moment Liz saw Dary's passive, withdrawn look change to a hard stare of fear. Liz turned to see Brad walking toward them. His truck was parked at the curb. Dary started running down the hill.

"Dary," Liz called. "Wait. Wait for me." But she didn't run after her, because she didn't want to leave Brad and Ben alone.

41

Brad looked angry. "Where's my money?" he yelled. "Where is it?"

Before either of them could get on with the business of the tire, Liz blurted out, "You scared Dary again, Brad. What did you say to frighten her? What did you *do*?" Did he try to get Dary to go in the truck with him when I wasn't around? she wondered angrily. Did he put his big paws on her? She realized that since Dary couldn't speak English she couldn't tell Liz if he had. Dary didn't know the words. And would she tell her strict aunt something like that?

"I didn't do nothin' to her," Brad said. He looked as if Dary had somehow hurt *his* feelings. "Man, you try to be nice and that's the thanks you get." He turned to Ben, glaring threateningly at him. "And you! You owe me ninety-six bucks, Chinaman. You ruined my tire."

Ben said calmly, "I don't know what you're talking about. I meant to ask you what that bill was all about when you handed it to me in school yesterday. I don't understand."

"You know what it's about, all right."

"No, I don't."

Brad shifted angrily from one foot to the other. "Just give me the money to buy a new tire and I'll forget it."

"Why should I pay for a new tire if I'm not responsible for whatever happened to the old one?"

Two of Brad's upperclassmen friends drove by, honking as they passed. "Get the chink," one of them called.

Brad grabbed Ben by the collar, lifted him off the ground, and threw him on the icy sidewalk. Ben landed with a thud.

Liz was ready to charge at Brad, to pound him. But Ben was already on his feet, handing his book bag to her. He crouched in a karate position, arms and hands in a rigid posture of readiness. Liz could see that Brad was surprised by Ben's threatening pose, but he was still ready to get into a fight with him.

42

"You sure you want to do this, Brad?" Ben asked in a cold, even voice. "It might be more sensible for both of us to wait until tomorrow. I promise that I'll settle up with you."

"That makes a lot of sense, Brad," Liz said. "I've known you for a long time. You've always been a fair guy. Tough, but fair."

Brad shuffled his feet like a restless bull. "Yeah. Tomorrow. And make it cash. I don't want a check." He looked at his watch. "I gotta go to work."

And he was gone.

"You were great," Liz told Ben. "How could you stay so calm? Do they teach you that in karate?"

"I don't know karate," Ben said. "Brad's such a racist he thinks all Asians know karate. He's seen too many kung fu movies." He winked at Liz. "You really thought I knew karate?"

"I don't know," Liz said. "You were pretty convincing."

Does he think I'm a dumb racist too? she wondered.

They waited in the grocery store across the street from the hardware store until they saw Brad's truck leaving with a delivery. "I don't get it," Liz told Ben as they crossed the street. "If Brad's got the truck how can we learn anything about the tire?"

"I went out to the parking lot at school during lunch hour and checked his tires," Ben explained. "He has two new back tires. We're after the old tire."

"How are we going to get it?"

Ben spoke in the low growl of a tough guy. "Just stick with me, babe, and follow my lead."

They went into the hardware store.

"Could we speak to the owner?" Ben asked the saleswoman. Liz followed Ben as he followed the saleswoman

43

down the narrow aisles past bins of nails and stacks of paint cans into Mr. Hadley's cramped office.

"Hi," Ben said as he leaned across the metal desk to shake hands. "I'm Benjamin Lee. And this is Elizabeth Gaynor." As Liz was shaking hands with Mr. Hadley she thought, we should be sleuthing, sneaking around looking for evidence. Instead we're acting like we're running for political office.

"Elizabeth and I are science students from the high school," Ben explained. "We're conducting a chemistry experiment in the composition of rubber. Do you have an old tire that you could spare for our research? We'd be happy to pay for it."

"Science class, huh? You people are great in math and science, aren't you? Always studying. I tell my kids, you want to get ahead, you've got to study like that. But for you oriental folks it comes real natural, doesn't it?"

Ben smiled pleasantly, but Liz suspected he was seething inside. She wondered how many times he'd heard that he was good in math and science because he was Asian.

"Elizabeth is my partner," Ben explained. "We're doing the rubber project together."

Liz smiled at Mr. Hadley. "We'd be so grateful if you could help us out."

"I'd like to: But this is a hardware store. We don't sell tires. You'd be better off at a garage."

"I was out back before," Ben told him, "and saw an old tire in the lumberyard. I guess that's what gave me the idea of asking you."

"Well, if it's there it's yours. Just check with my man in the back." He craned his neck to look out the window behind him. "Brad should be back pretty soon. Just ask him."

* * *

"Hurry," Ben said as they rushed out the back door toward the lumberyard.

"I suppose you saw the tire out here during your lunch hour too," Liz said.

"Just an educated guess."

They walked into the garage and there it was—an old, threadbare tire leaning against the wall.

As Ben carried it toward the door he told Liz to pick up any nails she saw lying around on the floor. She found three. By then Ben had discovered an alley to the street behind Hadley's and they were out of there.

They took turns rolling the tire to her house, walking fast the whole way. At the sound of every car Liz expected to see Brad drive by, catching them in the act of taking the old tire.

She didn't feel safe until they were in her kitchen. She took a final look out the window. No sign of Brad.

Ben bent over the tire. "Let's see what we've got here. Do you have a big container we could put water in? Something big enough to hold the tire?"

"The bathtub?" she suggested.

Ben had never been in her house before. And to get to the only bathroom with a bathtub in it you had to go through her bedroom.

"This is my room," she explained as they passed through. "It's a mess." She was annoyed with herself for not making her bed or putting away the clothes she'd worn the day before.

"It looks just like I imagined it would," Ben said.

What does that mean? Liz asked herself. Should I be embarrassed that this is what he thinks my room would look like—a disaster area? Or should I be flattered that he even thought about what it would look like?

The bathroom was also a mess. Towels, makeup, brushes, beauty aids scattered everywhere.

45

Ben leaned over the tub, plugged the drain, and turned on the cold water. "Can I use your phone?" he asked above the noise of the running faucet.

"Sure." She pointed through the open door to her bedroom. "There's one next to my bed."

"Turn off the water when the tub is a third full," he told her as he stood up. "I'll be right back."

He sat on her unmade bed to make his call. When Liz turned off the tap she could hear more clearly what he was saying. "It's for school, Mom. We're studying. I'll be home in an hour. I'm sorry I didn't call before." Then he spoke in Chinese. In the middle of what he was saying she heard "Joey."

Liz didn't need to understand Chinese in order to figure out that Ben was telling his mother that he was studying with Joey instead of with her. When he came back into the bathroom she wanted to ask, why couldn't you tell your mother that you're studying with me? But instead she said, "I thought you couldn't speak Chinese."

"I speak it a little," he admitted. "Sometimes at home. But I don't speak Khmer."

Ben lifted the tire. "Here, help me with this."

They put the tire into the tub. "Watch carefully," he said as he rolled it around.

"What are we looking for?"

"Bubbles. That'll show us where the leak is. Then we'll figure out how it got there."

"Why would there be bubbles if there's no air in the tire?" Liz asked.

Ben thought for a second then grunted, "Good point." He pulled the tub stopper to let the water drain, lifted the wet tire, put it on the bath mat. He smiled at her. "One clean tire, no evidence."

"I might have a magnifying glass," Liz said. "Should I look for it?"

"That's exactly what we need."

Half an hour later they were sitting next to one another at the kitchen table studying a one-foot chunk of tire and the few nails Liz had picked up at the lumberyard.

She looked up. Ben was staring at her.

"What's wrong?" she asked.

"Nothing."

"What were you thinking about just then?"

"How much I like working with you." He hesitated. "How much I like being with you."

Liz knew she was blushing like crazy when she said, "Me too."

They just looked at one another. Will he kiss me? Liz wondered.

The kitchen door opened and a cheery voice called out, "Well, hello there."

Before Liz could introduce Ben, her mother walked over to the table, gave Ben a big smile, and said, "You must be Ben Lee. How nice to finally meet you." Liz realized that her mother knew it was Ben and not another of her friends that she hadn't met because he was the only Asian American boy in her class.

Ben and Liz put away their "science project" while her mother started dinner. "Would you like to stay for dinner, Ben?" she asked. At least, Liz thought, she's treating him like she would any of my other friends. Then her mother added, "It's spaghetti. I don't know, do you eat Italian food?"

"I love Italian food," Ben said. "But I have to get home. My mother is expecting me."

Diane chuckled. "If this was Thursday we'd be eating take-out from your restaurant. It must be nice for your mother, having a restaurant. She doesn't have to cook. Unless she is the cook. In the restaurant, that is."

47

What is she going on about? Liz wondered. Why is she acting so rattled?

"My mother is the business manager of the restaurant," Ben explained. "She does the books. She cooks our meals at home."

"Somehow I pictured you all gathered around one of those booths in the back eating dinner."

"The waiters do that." Even though Ben was being respectful to her mother, Liz knew that this conversation was bothering him. It certainly was bugging her.

Liz's father came in. "Ben," he said as he extended his hand for a shake, obviously recognizing Liz's only Asian friend. "Nice to meet you."

A few minutes later Liz walked Ben to the front door. "I'm sorry," she said, "about how my mother acted. Sometimes she's weird with my friends."

"That's okay," Ben said. "I'm used to it. Everyone's parents do that. They have a certain idea about how Chinese people are. They never think of me as just another kid."

Liz went back to the kitchen to set the table. She was trying to figure out how to explain to her mother that she was rude to Ben, when her father said, "Well, we've finally met your competition."

"Ben's not my competition," Liz said. "He's my friend." She emphasized, "My good friend."

"We know, dear," her mother said. "But face it, you and Ben are neck and neck for the top class standing."

Her father looked up from the front page of the newspaper he'd been scanning. "You know what I think? I think there's a prejudice towards Ben."

"There is," Liz said. She was about to tell them about the way Brad and some of the other kids called Ben "chink" and "Chinaman." And how, in a way, her mother's behavior was insulting to Ben. But she didn't get a chance be-

cause her father kept talking. "I'm glad you recognize that, Elizabeth. It's a subtle prejudice, I'm sure. Maybe the teachers don't even realize they're doing it. The expectation now is that an Asian will do better in math and science than one of our own."

Remembering what Mr. Hadley said to Ben at the hardware store, Liz said, "A lot of people think that but—"

"That's right," her mother interrupted. "And they give him better grades because they expect him to do better than you. That's why so many Asians are walking away with all those science and math awards . . . and, I might add, scholarships. It's very unfair to you. And to American kids. You're the ones who suffer from the prejudice."

"That's crazy," Liz said. "That's not what I meant. It's not *me* they're prejudiced against. It's Ben. Everyone treats him like he's different when he's just another American kid."

"Is he?" her mother asked.

"Yes," Liz answered with a snap. "He is."

FIVE

Early the next morning Dary's aunt phoned Liz to say that Dary was sick with a cold and wouldn't be going to school. Liz was walking alone up the hill toward school when the bus passed. Ben knocked on the window and waved to her. At school he came to meet her.

Liz was happy but annoyed. If Dary had been with her, she knew, he wouldn't have met her. She wanted to ask him why. Instead she asked, "Are you ready for Brad?"

"Ready." He held up a brown shopping bag and shook it. The piece of hard rubber tire rattled inside. "I phoned him last night. Told him to meet me in the science lab at noon 'to settle up.' "

"He thinks you're going to pay him?"

"I am going to pay him. I'm going to pay him back for all his insults."

She put her hand on his sleeve. "Just be careful. Don't start anything with him. It's not worth it. He's not worth it."

Ben put his free hand over hers and held it for a second. "Don't worry," he said.

"I just don't want anyone to get hurt over this thing," Liz said.

Liz and Terry faced the long bathroom mirror over the row of five porcelain sinks in the second floor girls' room. "Joey can get his mother's car Saturday night," Terry announced. "We're going to Middlebury to a movie. We want to double-date with you." Terry smiled at Liz's reflection in the mirror. "Joey has an idea of who we could set you up with."

"Who?" Liz asked, hoping they'd finally thought of Ben.

Terry couldn't hold back the grin when she answered, "Brad Mulville."

Liz flicked a spray of water on Terry's reflection. "Very funny."

Terry lowered her voice so the girls in the stalls behind them wouldn't overhear. "Seriously. Joey said something about you to Alex Cranston. He said that Alex likes you."

Liz whispered back, "Alex Cranston's a stuck-up snob. I can't stand him."

As they left the bathroom and headed down the hall toward the cafeteria Terry asked, "Won't you even give it a try, Liz? I mean if Alex is willing to."

Elizabeth shook her head.

"Liz, Joey and I can't do any better than Alex. There has to be someone that you're interested in. Now come on. Tell me who it is."

"Ben."

"Ben Lee?"

"Yes."

Terry didn't say anything.

"What's wrong with that?" Liz challenged her.

"Nothing. I just think of you two more as intellectual buddies than a romantic couple. It never occurred to me."

"Why didn't it occur to you? I have a lot more in common with him than with any other guy around here."

"I don't know. I guess I just never thought about Ben being like the rest of us," Terry said. "I mean, I like him a lot, but he's so ambitious, with his brother at Harvard and everything."

"I'm ambitious too," Liz said.

"Yeah, but you're not headed for the Ivy League the way he is."

"I guess not. My parents have always been really big on my going to UVM."

"Not to mention the fact that he's Chinese."

"Is it so weird?" Liz knew she sounded defensive.

"Listen, don't get mad at me, okay? But he's different."

"The only difference I see," Liz said, "is that he's Chinese and I'm not."

"Either way you look at it," Terry said, "it's a new idea for Ethan Allen High." She put her arm around her friend. "But I say, if that's what you want, go for it."

A few minutes later as they were moving with the cafeteria line, Terry said, "Food, F-O-O-D."

"Bad food," Liz continued, "B-A-D."

"You're amazing," Terry said, "I don't know where you get the patience to work with Dary."

"She's trying so hard," Liz said as she picked up a plate of pretty b-a-d looking hot dogs and beans. "Imagine what it must be like for her not understanding anything. 'Globbidy Goo cearili po winicho.' "

"Is that her language?"

"No. But that's about as much sense as English must make to her."

Terry put a tuna salad plate on her tray. "I see what you mean."

"Hey, your boyfriend is waving to you," Liz told her as they moved off the cafeteria line.

Terry waved in Joey's direction. "Let's sit with him."

53

Liz felt her face flush. "Don't say anything to him in front of me about my thing about Ben."

"Whatever you say."

They headed toward the big table that Joey had staked out for them. "Where's Ben?" Terry asked as they put their trays on the table.

"He had to do something in the science lab." Joey patted a spot at the end of the table. "I'm saving him a place." He looked up at Liz. "You're his science partner. You didn't know that he was working in the lab during lunch hour?" Raising his eyebrows he whispered conspiratorially, "Maybe Ben is doing a secret project without you so he can soar ahead and win the science prize."

Liz sat in the chair next to the reserved space. She realized that Ben hadn't told Joey about the bill for the tire that Brad had given him. She thought of Ben and Brad alone in the lab. What would happen when Brad realized that Ben had no intention of paying for the tire? Would he get angry? What if he got so angry that he became violent? A fight with Brad could be a disaster for anyone. And if Brad's buddies were there to join in the fight it would be a triple disaster.

She stood up. "I just remembered I forgot something. I'll be right back."

"If you leave I'm telling Joey about what we were talking about in the bathroom," Terry said. "Okay?"

"Sure. Whatever you want."

"Telling me about what in the bathroom?" Joey asked Terry as Liz made her exit from the cafeteria.

Liz hurried along the short corridor to the lab. Even with the evidence of the flat tire and their experiments the day before, there had been no way of determining what had caused the flat. The nails that they'd picked up in the lumberyard didn't match the puncture hole, which meant

54

there was no way to prove Ben hadn't done it. So Ben was making up a scientific explanation to convince Brad that the flat came from a nail at the lumberyard.

Liz put her ear over the crack where the door met the doorjamb. She listened as Ben smoothly and authoritatively spewed forth pure nonsense. He was telling Brad about temperatures and velocity, and was throwing in some mathematical equations for good measure. Liz knew it was all jargon, with no meaning. Was Brad falling for this nonsensical explanation?

Finally Brad spoke. "Sure I understand. Man, what do you think, that I'm some kind of a jerk? I can see how that's what happened, man. You people think you're so smart no one else can understand nothin'."

"And it was a pretty old tire," Ben reminded him. "Every five hundred miles a tire like that loses a hundredth of a millimeter of tread, which raises the probability factor for a failure in endurance by a multiple of the velocity."

"Yeah. Of course," Brad said. "I heard about that."

So that's that, Liz thought as she headed back to the cafeteria.

Joey winked at her when she reached the table. "So how's Ben?" he asked.

"Fine, I guess." She scraped off the orangey yellow grease that had coagulated in beads on the length of her hot dog. Joey's always been a tease, she thought, but now that he knows I like Ben as a boyfriend, he'll probably drive me crazy.

By the time she'd decided not to eat the hot dog and had scooped the beans into the roll instead, Ben had joined them.

"How's it going?" Joey asked.

"All right," Ben answered. He looked right at Liz when he added, "Couldn't be better." But he didn't tell Joey what had happened with Brad.

"Hey Ben," Terry said as she gave Liz a little kick under the table, "Joey and I are going to Middlebury Saturday afternoon. We thought we'd catch a movie and have something to eat."

"You and Liz want to come with us?" Joey asked.

"Sounds good to me," Ben said. He turned to Liz. "Do you want to?"

Liz kicked Terry back when she said, "Fine with me." Her heart was racing, it would be their first date.

A few minutes later there was an explosion of laughter from across the room. They looked in the direction of one of the senior tables where Brad's upperclassmen sidekicks—Mike and Frank—sat with two girls. They all faced Brad, who was pulling up a chair at the foot of the table. They were practically jumping out of their seats with laughter. Brad looked thoroughly confused. Mike got up and put his arm around him. Mike was trying to speak, but couldn't through the rush of guffaws.

Joey was on his feet. "Come on," he said. "Let's see what's going on. What's Brad got in his hand?"

Liz and Ben exchanged a worried glance as they followed Joey and Terry. Brad was holding the piece of tire.

"What's wrong with you guys?" they heard Brad ask Mike.

"It's just . . . I mean . . ." Mike couldn't go on.

Brad yelled, "Would you stop laughing? Don't you understand? It's scientific. That's how it happened."

"It's nonsense," someone at another table yelled out.

"Oh, no," Liz whispered to Ben. "You better get out of here." But it was too late.

"There he is." Brad was pointing to Ben. "Hey come over here. Tell 'em how it happened."

Everyone watched Ben walk toward Brad.

"What's going on?" Joey asked Liz. "Is Brad still on that tire business?"

Liz nodded.

"Your tire probably rolled over a nail in the lumberyard," Ben said. "So you got a flat."

"Probably?" Brad said. "Tell them all that stuff about the velocity and that math business."

Ben checked out who was listening and decided that he couldn't get away with the nonsensical scientific explanation he'd given Brad. There were a lot of kids who would see right through it.

"Man," Mike said, "don't you get it, buddy? He was pulling your leg."

"Pulling his brain would be more like it," someone called out.

Brad shook off Mike's arm and moved toward Ben.

"I didn't go near your tire," Ben said.

Brad waved the piece of tire at him. "What do you call this?"

"I mean before it was flat," Ben added quickly. He didn't back away as Brad approached him, but everyone else in the crowd was making room for what Brad's reddening face and tensing body were showing: There would be a fight.

"What's going on here?" Mr. Madison pushed through the circle that had formed around the two boys and put himself between them. He glared at Brad. "You stirring something up here, Brad? You're on probation as it is."

"I didn't do nothin'," Brad yelled. "Nothin'. That yellow bastard. He's the one who did something." Brad wound up and threw the square of hard rubber at Ben's head. Everyone gasped as Ben ducked in time to have it bounce off his shoulder instead of hitting him full across the face.

Mr. Madison put a strong grip on Brad's arm. "Let's go, Mr. Mulville."

In the wake of Brad's loud complaints as Mr. Madison led him away, Mike shook his head and chortled to the crowd, "That guy just can't win."

Ben leaned closer to Liz and whispered, "I'm going to the office and straighten this out."

"I'll go with you."

He shook his head. "I'll take care of it."

A few kids applauded as Ben passed them. "Smooth move, Ben," someone called out. "You really had him going there."

A minute later as Liz was placing her tray on the cleanup conveyor belt she overheard one of the senior girls tell her boyfriend, "That Chinese kid's got guts pulling something like that on Brad."

"Either that or he's really dumb," the boyfriend rejoined.

Liz wondered which of them was right. She also wondered what was going on in the principal's office. She was still wondering at eight o'clock when she picked up the phone and, for the first time in her life, telephoned Ben Lee.

A woman—Liz guessed that it was Ben's mother—answered on the third ring.

"Hello," Liz said. "Is Ben there?"

"Who is this calling please?"

"Elizabeth Gaynor. I'm a classmate of Ben's"

With a finality that meant *He's not to be disturbed*, Mrs. Lee said, "Ben is studying."

Ben came into the living room as his mother was saying this. "Is the phone for me?" he asked.

Tia Lee turned and looked at her son. "Did not want to disturb you," she explained.

"I should take it," he said, "if someone went through the trouble of calling."

"It's a girl," she said. "Named Elizabeth Gaynor."

58

"Elizabeth and I are lab partners in the science class," he explained.

"A girl?"

"Yes. We're doing a science project and need to talk about it." He took the receiver from his mother and put it to his ear. "Hello, Elizabeth."

Liz, having overheard most of the conversation at the other end, said, "I guess I shouldn't have called."

"That's all right."

"I was worried. After what happened in the cafeteria and then I didn't see you the rest of the day."

"I had a lot of explaining to do." Because his mother was right there he added, "About that rubber experiment."

"How did the Brad factor work out?"

"I can explain that problem to you tomorrow."

Since a guessing game seemed to be the only way Liz had for getting information, she asked, "Is Brad suspended?"

"Yes."

"For how long?"

"A week."

"What about you? You weren't suspended were you? I mean you didn't do anything wrong. Not really."

"You've got that part totally correct," he answered.

Remembering how unfriendly his mother was to her on the phone, Liz asked, "Did your parents have to go to school or anything?"

"No." Ben turned and smiled at his mother where she sat listening to his end of the conversation. "That is a result that should be avoided at all costs . . . in this experiment."

There was a pause.

"Ben," Liz said, "if Brad was suspended he must be so angry at you."

"Yes," Ben said.

As Liz was telling him how some of the kids in the

59

cafeteria had reacted to the incident with Brad, Ben looked around the living room. They lived in a small New England woodframe house but his mother had done everything she possibly could to make it look Chinese. And she cooked only Chinese-style food. She had lived in America for twenty years but her ways were totally Chinese—which meant that she considered dating only as a route to marriage and that her son's wife must be Chinese. Any other possibility was unthinkable. So Ben knew—as he listened to the lovely voice of the girl who, of all the girls he'd known, he was most attracted to—that somehow he must keep his relationship with Elizabeth a secret from his parents.

His mother said—in Chinese—"It's time to get off the phone to study."

"I have to go now," Ben told Elizabeth. "My mother is expecting me to do something for her."

Liz hung up. As she walked around her room, reconstructing the bizarre conversation in her head, she wondered why Ben hadn't told his mother before that she was his science lab partner. And why was he so formal on the phone? At least, she thought, my parents know Ben and I are friends. She figured Ben's mother would be pretty upset if she knew her son had a date with a Caucasian girl. Then, for the first time, she wondered what her parents' reaction would be when they found out she was going on a date with a Chinese American boy.

The next morning Ben found Liz at the lockers. "I explained the whole situation to Mrs. Harmon. How Brad blamed me for his flat and that I had to find a way to get him off my back."

"What did Brad say?"

"He said that he was more sure than ever that I'd flattened his tire, that I was sneaky. That didn't Mrs. Harmon know how sneaky 'those kind' are?"

"He said that to Mrs. Harmon, in front of you?"

"And worse. There I was trying to defuse the situation. I even apologized for making him look stupid, but he kept saying these racist things about me. If he'd kept his big mouth shut he wouldn't have been suspended."

"So they suspended him for his racist comments?"

"Not just that. Throwing that piece of rubber was a real no-no. And they found a knife on him."

"He had a knife? In school? That's pretty scary."

"He said it was for work."

"At least he didn't throw it."

Ben grinned. "I guess I got a little carried away with my scientific explanation. But the more he believed me, the more I went on. It was like he was asking for it. How could anybody be so dumb?"

"Maybe you're just very smart," Liz said.

"Not smart enough. Brad still thinks I gave him a flat tire."

"He also thinks you know karate."

That evening, Liz's parents were sitting in the living room watching the late news when she passed through on her way to the kitchen. She'd promised herself that if she finished the reading assignment in the novel *Pride and Prejudice* she would reward herself with a cold roast chicken leg. She'd finished the reading and the leg was calling to her. But so was her mother. "Elizabeth," she yelled over the big-band music of a car commercial, "Saturday when I finish work let's go shopping for some spring clothes. Bright, cheery, lightweight clothes. I'm so sick of winter."

"Saturday?" Her date with Ben was starting at three o'clock in the afternoon. "I'm busy. Sorry. How about the next Saturday?"

She went into the kitchen. I better tell them about Ben, she thought as she opened the refrigerator and pulled out the chicken leg. She sat at the table. Her mother came in and sat in front of her. "Can't you change your plans? I'd really like to do it this Saturday. The mood is on me. If you're doing something with Terry let her come along." Her mother brightened. "I'll take you both to a late lunch. What do you say?"

"Mom, I have a date Saturday. In fact I'm double-dating with Terry and Joey. They're going out together now. We're going to Middlebury to a movie. I mean if it's okay with

you and Dad." She smiled at her mother. "I'll be back by ten."

"It depends on who the young man is," her mother said. "Is it the one who sent you that Valentine's Day card?"

"No. I'm going with Ben Lee."

"Oh, well, you four kids hang out together all the time." She stood up to get back to the news. "I just wish you weren't doing it when I wanted to go shopping with you."

She doesn't get it, Liz thought. "But it's not just to hang out together, Mom. I really like him."

"I thought you always really liked him."

"I did. But now I really like him like a boyfriend."

"Oh," Diane said. After a pause she asked, "Does he like you like a girlfriend?"

"I think so."

"Then, well, good." Diane was determined not to seem too surprised or the least bit upset. So what if her daughter had a Chinese boyfriend? She was only fifteen. It wasn't as if they were getting married. Besides Ben Lee was intelligent, well-mannered, clean. Why, he proably was a perfect first romance for her daughter. And since he was academically oriented he wouldn't distract Liz from her schoolwork.

"Hey, honey," Tom Gaynor yelled from the living room. "The news is back."

"Well that's splendid, dear," Diane said to Liz as she got up from the chair. "You should have Ben over for dinner sometime." At the doorway she turned and added, "But the following Saturday let's shop."

Later, when Liz was back in her room and Diane and Tom had turned off the television, Diane told him about Ben Lee. "What do you think?" she asked.

"I think the less we say about it—to her, that is—the better. It won't last, honey. I mean, not long enough to

make it a problem. Look at it this way: It won't interfere with her schoolwork."

"But I'm afraid helping this girl Dary will," Diane commented.

"We'll see how long that lasts too."

On the way to Middlebury Ben and Liz told Terry and Joey the whole "Brad and the Tire" incident. Joey laughed so hard that he had to take off his sunglasses and wipe his eyes. "You two wheeled an old tire around town, put it in the bathtub, and cut it up, and still you couldn't prove anything? Don't ever open a detective agency."

After the story they all settled back to enjoy the good feeling of being together—the four of them. Two girls who were best friends. Two guys who were also friends. And now two couples. Pretty perfect, Liz thought. In the front seat Terry shifted as close to Joey as her seat belt would allow. In the back when a sharp curve slid Liz's knee close to Ben's neither of them moved to break the charged contact. Terry had brought along some of her homemade music tapes. They listened to a tape that Terry called "Valentine" because every song had the word love in it and she put it together the day after the Valentine's Day dance that marked the beginning of her romance with Joey.

In Middlebury they went directly to the theater. About halfway through the movie, Ben took Liz's hand in his. Their hands rested comfortably together. When the movie got scary they held on tight, squeezing. During the calmer moments of the story and during the happy ending, Ben gently rubbed the palm of her hand with his thumb. Liz didn't know if she'd ever been this happy in her whole life.

When the movie let out it was dark. And cold. The sky was clear and studded with stars. "What now?" Terry asked.

"I know about this diner," Joey said, "near the college

where lots of the Middlebury College students hang out. Want to go there?"

They all agreed.

"We'll probably fit right in," Terry commented as the four of them headed to the Sidelines Diner. "I mean, how would anyone know we're high school students and not college students? If anyone asks, I'm going to say I'm a sophomore. I just won't say in high school."

We do fit in, Liz thought as they settled into their booth. She saw that of the fifty or so customers in the noisy, brightly lit diner, at least ten were Asian Americans. She wondered if Ben noticed, and realized that of course he must have. Did Terry and Joey? No one mentioned it. Of those Asians, the one that interested Liz the most was the boy with a Caucasian girl. You could tell they were girlfriend and boyfriend. Is that what Ben and I look like together? she wondered. "I like it here," she told the others. "Isn't it great?"

They all had burger platters and large colas. Joey ordered a chocolate milkshake, which they shared. As Liz took a sip of the thick milk through her straw she thought of Dary and wondered how long it would be before Dary would know enough English and have the friends so that she could have a wonderful time like Liz was having.

After eating at the diner they strolled hand in hand, two by two, along the campus walks.

"College is going to be great," Ben told Liz. "I can't wait."

"Are you going to UVM?" She hoped against hope he'd say yes, that they'd be in college together too. But Terry was probably right. Ben was the ambitious type who'd want to go to an Ivy League school.

"I don't know where I'm going yet," he told Liz.

"I've always thought I'd go to UVM. I guess because my

parents have always said that's where I should go." For the first time it occurred to Liz that maybe her parents underestimated her.

"But you should check out different schools," he told her, "so you have a choice. I stayed with my brother at Harvard. I even sat in on his classes."

"Is that where you'd like to go?" Liz asked.

"Maybe," Ben said. "I'm looking at several schools, so I can see what's best for me. I'll visit all of them before I apply."

Liz thought, he sounds so confident, like he can have his pick of schools. Like the idea of going to Harvard—Harvard!—is totally reasonable. Well, why not? He certainly has the grades. I do too, she suddenly realized. I do too. I could go to Harvard too!

They stopped in front of the library and looked up at the old building with its modern extensions stretched out like arms. Through brightly lit windows they watched students walking around the stacks or working at tables and in study carousels.

"They're open on Saturday night!" Joey exclaimed. "That's disgusting. Saturday night is party night."

Ben said, "Let's go in."

Terry turned to him. "No way am I going into another library. The research for that last history paper did me in."

Ben leaned closer to Liz and whispered, "I love libraries."

"Me too," she agreed.

When they drove into Rutland it was almost ten o'clock. "Joey," Ben asked, "could you drop me off first? I told my parents I'd be home at ten. You could just drop me at the corner of Lincoln and North." Ben looked at Liz. "I'm sorry. I wish I could bring you home."

"I can drop you at your door," Joey told him.

"No, that's okay," Ben said quickly. "The corner is fine."

66

"But it's on the way. I have to—" Joey stopped mid-sentence. They all realized at the same instant that Ben hadn't told his parents that he was out with them. What had he told them? Liz wondered angrily. That he was studying? That he was at school or the library?

"This is fine," Ben said as Joey stopped at the corner curb. Ben took Liz's hand and kissed her on the lips. "Thanks for a great time. See you in school on Monday." Then to Joey, "Could you open the trunk? My books."

They drove past Ben, his backpack of schoolbooks over his shoulder, no one saying anything.

Ben must really be embarrassed, Joey thought, especially in front of Liz.

Terry felt sorry for Liz and glad that Joey wasn't like Ben.

This is so weird, Liz thought, after we had such a great time tonight. Are his parents so strict that they won't even let him go out on the weekend? Is this what dating Ben is going to be like? Do I want a boyfriend who has to sneak around to see me?

CHAPTER

SEVEN

Sunday mornings were lazy affairs at the Gaynors'. Liz's father usually made a late breakfast of waffles or french toast—his two specialties. The three of them sat around the table for at least an hour eating and reading the newspapers.

Usually Liz enjoyed the routine. Her father, with his blue and white striped apron, saying, "I aim to please." Her mother in her pink bathrobe, saying, "I love Sundays." But this morning Liz wasn't in the mood to be sociable. She picked at the waffle on her plate and hoped that her parents wouldn't ask too many questions about her date with Ben. She was still trying to figure it out herself.

"What's the matter, honey?" her father asked. "You're usually on your second waffle by now. I hope it's not my cooking."

"No, Dad, the waffle's great. I'm just not very hungry this morning."

"You're not on some crazy diet, are you?" her mother asked.

"No, I'm not on a diet. I'm just not very hungry today, okay?"

"Okay." Diane decided to change the subject with the usual Sunday morning question. "What's your day going to be like, honey?"

As always, both Liz and her father thought they were the "honey" of the question and both answered.

"I'm going over to the store to catch up on some inventory records," her father said.

"Dary's coming over today," Liz said. "Remember? I'm going to help her with her English."

Diane gave Tom a glance. "Right. Your service credit. But what about your own homework?"

"I'm caught up."

"But there's always studying for the SATs," her father commented. "Weren't you going to put some extra time in vocabulary?"

"I have. I'm only helping her for a few hours. I think it's more important for Dary to learn how to speak a simple sentence than it is for me to know the meaning of words I'll never use. Don't you?"

"Don't get huffy, young lady," her father admonished. "No one's arguing with you. It was a simple question."

"I'm not arguing. I'm just explaining."

Diane shot Tom a look that meant *Let's talk about something else* and turned to her daughter. "You haven't told us about your date last night. Did you have a good time?"

"Yeah. It was fun."

"Well," her father remarked, "I sure like a boy who has a ten o'clock curfew. A father's dream."

"That was just last night, Dad. It's not going to be like that all the time." Or is it? Liz wondered. If his parents were that strict, would there even be a next time?

When the doorbell rang half an hour later Liz opened the

door to find Dary standing shyly next to a man who bowed toward Elizabeth. "I am Mr. Dahm, Dary's uncle. Thank you for being help to Dary in English."

Liz inclined her body forward, answering his bow with a slight bow of her own. "Hello. Would you like to come in?"

"No thank you. In two hours I come in car for Dary." He said something in Khmer to his niece then said good-bye to Liz with another little bow and left.

Liz noticed that Dary was stiff and self-conscious as she walked through the living room toward the kitchen to be introduced to Liz's parents. No wonder, Liz thought. This is probably the first American home that Dary's been in. After they said their hellos, Liz led her friend upstairs. Dary, neatly dressed in her school skirt and a fresh white blouse, stood stiffly in the middle of Liz's room.

"Don't be so nervous," Liz told her. "This is a happy time. Like playing." And to prove she meant it, she turned on the radio. She tapped the machine. "Radio." Then as she spelled it out loud she wrote "R-A-D-I-O" on a blue Post-it and stuck it to the radio. Dary repeated "Radio."

Liz, moving to the beat of the music, went to her desk and slapped it. "What is it?" she asked Dary.

Dary hesitated, then remembered and said, "Desk." They spelled the word together as Liz wrote "D-E-S-K" on another blue Post-it.

In half an hour all the objects in Liz's room were labeled. Most were new words for Dary, but some like *window, door*, and *chair* were review words. Blue stickers dotted the room.

A knock on the door. Liz's mother came in with a tray of sodas and a dish of peanuts. "My goodness," she said, "it looks like a tag sale in here."

71

"Mother," Liz told Dary as she wrote out "M-O-T-H-E-R" on a blue Post-it. When her mother leaned over to put down the tray Liz stuck the Post-it to her forehead. Diane laughed. "It's dangerous in here," she declared as she made a quick exit.

That was when Liz saw one of Dary's infrequent smiles turn into a real laugh. She was still laughing as Liz put stickers on "S-O-D-A" and "P-E-A-N-U-T-S" and "T-R-A-Y."

After they had their snack Dary held her stomach. Oh no, Liz thought, what's she allergic to now? She hoped it wasn't the peanuts. Dary had eaten exactly twenty-seven of them, counting the numbers as she ate.

"Are you sick?" Liz asked. "Like you were in school?"

"No," Dary answered. "Like water."

Liz led her to the bathroom but left her there only after she'd labeled "T-O-I-L-E-T," "S-I-N-K," and "T-U-B."

When Dary came back into the bedroom the blue Post-its were gone. She looked around questioningly. Liz smiled and handed her the whole pile. "Put them on and say the word," she directed and demonstrated by putting the Post-it that said "D-O-O-R" on the tray.

Dary removed it. "No way," she said as she went to the door and placed the Post-it squarely in the middle of it. "Door."

Liz laughed too. *No way?* Where did Dary learn that?

Soon, with only a few errors and some practice in pronunciation, the room was again correctly labeled.

Now they needed some verbs, some action words. Liz opened the pack of pink Post-its. How would she do this?

She took a blue sticker, wrote "L-I-Z" on it, and stuck it to her sweatshirt. Then she made one that said "D-A-R-Y"

to put on Dary's blouse. She picked up her glass of soda with its "S-O-D-A" sticker and as she put it to her mouth said, "Liz drinks soda." After she took a sip, she wrote "D-R-I-N-K" on a pink Post-it. "Get it?" she asked Dary. She made the gesture again. "Drink."

Dary repeated "Drink," picked up a peanut, ate it, and said, "Dary drink peanut."

Liz said, "No way," and wrote "E-A-T" on another Post-it. "Dary *eats* a peanut."

In the next half hour, marked by pink Post-its, Dary learned to "close the door," "close the window," "close the mouth," "open the door," "open the window," "open the mouth," "throw the ball," and "throw the tray."

Then the two of them practiced, with action, "stand," "walk," "run," and "jump."

Liz put the radio back on. On a pink Post-it she wrote "D-A-N-C-E." She shouted above the music, "I love to dance. Liz dances," as she danced rock and roll–style all around the room. And for the second time Dary laughed. Liz grabbed her hand and gave it a gentle pull. "Dary dances."

Dary resisted with a firm "No way" and sat herself on the edge of the bed. Liz picked up her handsome brown teddy bear in his red-checked overalls and danced around with him. "Teddy bear," Liz said.

"Teddy bear boyfriend?" Dary asked.

"Yes," Liz said. "You bet."

Liz stopped. Now they were both laughing. "Dance more," Dary said.

Liz shook her head. She turned off the radio. "We need more words. Color words."

She took Dary over to her desk. They sat together in front of a box of Magic Markers and a big art pad. Dary already

knew some colors and the ones that she didn't know she learned fast. They wrote the names of the colors on yellow Post-its and Dary went around the room labeling the colors of things. Blue Post-its for nouns, pink Post-its for verbs, yellow Post-its for adjectives. As Liz watched Dary put "R-E-D," "G-R-E-E-N," and "W-H-I-T-E" on the rose-patterned curtains, she wondered how Dary would ever be able to cram all these words in her head. Would she remember them tomorrow?

The doorbell rang. "It must be your uncle," Liz said. "But wait. Homework." Liz grabbed a folder that she'd stuffed full of pages from old magazines for Dary. On each page Liz had affixed a blank white sticker. "Look," she said, showing Dary the picture of a teenage girl modeling a pair of jeans, standing near a tree. "Girl stands," Liz said as she wrote the sentence on the white sticker.

"Blue dress," Dary said, pointing to the jeans. "Be-au-tiful dress."

"More words." Liz pointed to Dary's skirt and said, "Skirt." She patted her own dungareed leg for "jeans," and pointed to a woman in a perfume ad for "dress."

"There are many words for clothes," Liz said.

Dary looked discouraged. "Much words. No way."

"Liz," her mother was calling up the stairs, "Mr. Dahm is here to pick up Dary."

"We're coming," she yelled to her mother. Dary turned to leave.

"No," Liz said. "Wait. Words are beautiful. You're learning very fast." She pointed to Dary's head. "You're very smart. You already know many words." She handed Dary the folder of magazine pages and Post-its. "I'm going to give you homework. Okay?"

"Okay." Dary took the folder and formally bowed toward Liz. "Thank you, friend." She held the folder carefully in both hands like it was of great value.

They went down the stairs and Liz watched through the window as Dary, talking animatedly to her uncle in Khmer, went to the car. Dary learned many words today, Liz thought.

"Well." Her mother was sitting on the couch behind her. "How did it go?"

"Pretty good."

"She seems like a very nice girl. Shy though. What country did you say she comes from?"

"Cambodia." Liz sat in the chair facing her mother and threw her legs over the side. "I didn't even know where it was so I looked it up in the atlas. It's right next to Vietnam."

"Cambodia was a real victim of the Vietnam War. I remember when your uncle Barry was in Vietnam we would read everything about it that we could find and Cambodia was a name that kept appearing in the news. It was really dragged into the war because of what was happening next door in Vietnam. Then after the war Cambodia went through a terrible civil war of its own. Haven't you studied that in American History?"

"We're only on World War II."

"From what I gather, it was a pretty bad situation. Your friend must have gone through a lot."

"Dary was probably only three or four years old during the war."

"Are her parents here?"

Liz shook her head. "I think she came alone. She lives with her aunt and uncle and some cousins. But they've been here for a few years."

"I wonder if she's been in one of those refugee camps.

It's amazing that they found her and got her out. Didn't she tell you about it?"

"Mom, she's just learning English. I don't know anything about her. She can't really talk yet."

"Well it's nice that you're being her friend."

"There's so much to teach her about English," Liz mused. "How am I ever going to get her to know about things like when to put s's on words? And what about the past and future tenses? And then there are prepositions and—"

"Hey, wait a minute here." Her mother sat up straight and leaned forward toward Liz. "The school is responsible for teaching her English. Not you. You're responsible for your own education. You've got enough to do studying to keep your grades up. You've done plenty for Dary already." She studied her daughter. "Look at you. You're all worn out and discouraged from working with her today. Teaching someone a language is hard work. This isn't your problem. Do you understand?"

Liz got out of the chair. "Yeah, I understand." What I understand, she thought, is that you don't think I can handle doing two things at the same time. "I'm going to go do my own work now." She turned when she was halfway up the stairs and called, "I don't mind helping her, Mom. Don't make such a big deal out of it, okay?"

"I'm just thinking about you, sweetie," her mother called back.

When she got to her room Liz took out her history book, lay across her bed, and read all she could find on Cambodia. Then she got up, went over to the globe on her desk and spun it around and around. A civil war: That was nothing less than a holocaust. Now she remembered she'd seen it dramatized in a movie. It was horrible. Butchery carried out by the Khmer Rouge, a guerilla group of young men led by Pol

76

Pot. Pol Pot's plan was to clean out their society of all the old ways of thinking and they did it by killing anyone who was educated or owned anything. If you wore glasses, had books, owned property, they'd kill you. Watching the movie had made her sick to her stomach. They'd murdered teachers, doctors, peasants, young and old.

She stopped the globe and put her finger over the little patch of orange that was labeled Cambodia. Over a million people murdered. Death squads. Killing fields. How little she knew about Dary. Did Dary have sisters and brothers who had died over there? Were her parents dead? What was her story? Would she ever know enough English to tell Liz about it? Would she ever want to?

By the time the church tower clock struck five o'clock Brad had been driving around town in his pickup truck for an hour, looking for someone to hang out with and for something to do. Buddy and Mike were with their girlfriends and he realized after being at Buddy's for a few minutes that they didn't really want him around. He went over to Sewards but the only people there were tired parents with their noisy kids having a Sunday dinner of burgers and shakes.

Brad cranked up the music on the car radio and made a turn on Town Line Road. He needed a girl, someone to go out with, someone to be with who was nice and pretty. Someone like Liz. They'd been good friends before high school, so why not now? I could have had her, he thought, if that chink hadn't messed things up for me. He pressed down on the gas pedal. First the chink took the girl he liked. Then the guy made him look stupid in front of everyone—including Liz. Why, Brad asked himself, couldn't he stay in his own country and leave me alone?

He put more pressure on the gas pedal as he took Merkin's Hill and thought about what he could do to get Liz to like him more. She's smart, he figured, so I bet she'd go for me if I was good in school. She'd have to like me better than some yellow foreigner.

I'll try, he resolved as he sped along. I'll go home now and study. I'll really try and then she'll like me. Then he remembered that he was suspended for a week. He remembered the defeated look in his mother's eyes and the slump in his father's shoulders when they sat in the principal's office for the millionth time and were told that their son was in trouble again. Well, he would study all week long. Then he'd be ready when he got back. He'd show everybody. He was sick of everyone thinking he was stupid.

The music was so loud that Brad didn't hear the siren of the state police car. It was the flashing red light dancing off the surface of his rearview mirror that finally got his attention. He glanced at the speedometer. Seventy-five. He pulled over for his second speeding ticket in less than a month. He gripped the steering wheel. He really couldn't do anything right. He really must be as stupid as everyone thought.

Ben came into the kitchen. "What's for dinner?" he asked.

Tia Lee looked up from the chopping board and smiled at her handsome son. "For you velvety corn soup and spicy chicken."

Ben laughed. "For me? What about you and Dad and Uncle Trini?"

"But you're the one I think of, because I see that you have studied very hard all day." She went back to her chopping.

"It seems all I ever do is study," Ben said.

"That's why we work so hard in America," his mother

reminded him. "For you to have the opportunity for a very good education."

"I know. And I am grateful. But I don't need to be home all the time. My friends do well in school and they don't have to study all weekend. They're allowed to go out and they don't have to be in at ten o'clock either." He remembered how he hadn't told his parents he had a date on Saturday night and how when he was rushing to get home by ten he had Joey drop him off at the corner. Liz had such a surprised and disappointed look in her eyes when he said good night that he'd felt mortified. What did she think of him now?

"You see your friends plenty. You went to the dance on Valentine's Day. I don't think you have so much fun with these American children. You came home early from the dance."

" 'These American children!' Mom, I'm an American. I've never lived in China."

"You come from a Chinese family."

"Yes, but we live in America. Everything I know is American. So I want to do what the Americans—I mean, what *we* Americans—do. And not have everything be so strict."

"It seems to me that you already are an American," his mother commented as she regarded him critically. "You are talking back to me just like one of them." She went back to her chopping. Clearly their conversation was over.

"I'm sorry, Maman," he said.

Back in his room he flipped through last year's yearbook. His first year in Rutland and at Ethan Allen High. Freshman class. He looked over the row of faces. All different. Some with dark hair, some with light, some tall, some short, fat ones and skinny ones. There were smiling faces, shy expressions, and one or two who looked bored. But

one face stood out from the others as being the most different—his face.

He went into the bathroom and looked at his reflection in the medicine chest mirror. He could never just mix in and look like everyone else. No matter how American his tastes, interests, and views, he'd always be "that Chinese boy." The chink. No number of burger platters, pairs of jeans, rented videos, or dates with Caucasian girls would change that.

He stared at his face. The skin people called yellow seemed to him to be more brownish than yellow. And why did they call him "slant-eyes"? His eyes weren't slanted; they looked like regular eyes to him. Maybe they said that because his eyes were small. But lots of people had small eyes; that didn't make you Chinese. He leaned closer to his own image and felt the ridge between his eyes with his forefinger. Do I really have more space there than Caucasians, he wondered, or does it look that way because of the way my eyelids fold? He wished for a second that he could change his face. Then he dropped his hands and turned from his reflection. His shame made him feel sick to his stomach.

Monday at lunch Liz sat with Dary and corrected the homework she'd given her on the magazine tear-outs. Terry was eating lunch with Joey, and Ben was with two other guys. Liz found herself looking in Ben's direction. She had wanted to ask him about his ten o'clock curfew on Saturday and why he'd had to tell his parents that he was studying instead of being on a date with her. But she didn't know how to bring up the subject without embarrassing him. At that moment Ben looked up and smiled at her so sweetly that she didn't care about Saturday. They exchanged charged glances. Come over, she mouthed to him, but he shook his head and resumed his conversation.

Just before the bell, Ben came over to her table. Liz knew that he hadn't come over that whole time because of Dary and for the ten thousandth time she wondered why.

"How you doing?" Ben asked.

"Okay."

Dary looked up from the sentence she was printing to see who'd sat down at their table. "Hi," Ben said. "How's it going?"

"Hi," Dary answered with a shy smile.

"While you study," Liz told her, "I'm going to talk fast to Ben."

"You bet," Dary said and bent over her work. Ben wondered if that was how it was for his parents when they first came to America. Like Dary they had been teenagers who didn't know any English when they arrived, and like her they had to learn it word by word. But my parents didn't go to school, Ben recalled. They learned the language as they worked in laundries and restaurants.

Liz broke the silence. "Have you decided which topic you'll use for your paper on *Pride and Prejudice*?" she asked.

"I think I'll compare the movie and the book. What about you?"

Liz smiled. "Me too."

"Did you see the movie yet?" Ben asked.

"No, but I've got the videotape. My mother loves that movie so she taped it off television." Liz hesitated. "You want to watch it with me after school or something? Then we could talk about it." She hoped she wasn't being too forward.

"Sure. Watching movies for homework sounds great to me." He laughed.

"When do you want to do it?" she asked. "Today? Tomorrow?"

"I was going to do the paper next week."

"So why don't we watch the movie Sunday afternoon? I mean, if you want. My parents won't mind."

My parents will mind, Ben thought. But he said, "That'd be great."

As he was leaving Liz pictured herself with Ben, alone in the den, next to one another on the couch. So did Ben.

When Liz's phone rang at eight o'clock she had the feeling that it was Ben. That's what love's like, she thought, as she sat on the edge of her bed and picked up the receiver— you *know* it's he who's calling.

She almost answered the phone with a "Hi, Ben." She was that sure. But since she didn't want him to know she was that sure, she just said "Hello."

"Hi, Liz," the male voice on the other end said. "It's me, Brad."

It took her a second to accept who was on the other line. Finally she said, "Oh, Brad." Brad had never, ever called her. Unless you counted the prank phone calls about Prince Albert in a can and the running refrigerator when they were in fourth grade. What could he want?

"I'm not in school this week," he said. He sounded nervous.

Please, Liz prayed, please don't mention the Valentine's Day card. Please don't ask me out on a date.

"I know."

"It's that Chinese guy's fault. He got me in trouble." Brad bit his lower lip to keep from saying any more about Ben. This wasn't why he'd called her.

"Ben didn't do anything to your tire, Brad." She wanted to add, why can't you get that through your stupid, bigoted head? Instead she said, "He doesn't want any trouble."

Then why is he messing with me? Brad wanted to ask

her. Why is he making a fool out of me in front of everybody? Aloud he said, "That's not why I called."

Here it comes. Liz cringed inwardly. He's going to ask me out.

"What I called about was the homework. Because I'm not in school I wondered what I had to do to keep up."

Keep up, Liz thought. How about ten years' worth of school. "What's that got to do with me?"

"Maybe you could give me the homework for English and history. Those are the two classes we're in together."

"Ah, sure. You got a paper and pencil?"

"Just a minute." Where was a piece of paper and a pencil? Of course he needed to be able to write down what he had to do. Why hadn't he thought of that?

He frantically searched through the pockets of his denim jacket—he must have a pencil stashed there somewhere. He finally came up with a pencil—was it the one Liz had lent him that one time she had sat next to him?—and grabbed the paperback novel Mr. Madison had assigned. He could write on the inside of the cover. "Okay," he told Liz. "I'm all set."

Liz had moved with the phone over to her desk. "In history we're reading chapter four and doing the questions at the end. I guess we'll get through five and six this week. She's showing a film, some documentary, on the Eastern Front on Friday. I guess you'll miss that."

"Will you take notes on it?" Brad asked.

"On what?"

"The movie."

"I guess."

"So maybe I could look at them. Or you could tell me what it's about."

Oh no, Liz thought, what is going on here?

That's perfect, Brad congratulated himself, asking her to show me her notes. "What about English?"

"Well we have to finish *Pride and Prejudice* this week and we're discussing it in class. The same way we did the first part."

Brad turned over the cover of the book in which he was writing his assignments and looked at it. *Pride and Prejudice*. He had tried to read it. All day he'd tried. But it was hard and he couldn't understand much that was going on in it. He wished he'd paid more attention to the class discussions.

"Instead of a test," Liz continued, "Mr. Madison gave out a sheet with ideas for essays. We have to choose one. There're seven topics to choose from." She looked at the page. Each question had five or six parts. It would take forever to dictate them. "Why don't you just get a copy from Mr. Madison?" she suggested.

"I can't go to school. I'm suspended. Maybe you could get it for me and I'll come by your place after you get home from school to pick it up."

"No," Liz said quickly. "I'll read all the questions and then you copy down the one you think you'll use." She couldn't remember ever seeing Brad turn in a paper. Still, she read the list, including the question that compared the book and the 1940 film.

"There's a movie of this book?" Brad said. "Hey, great." What a relief. He could rent the movie and wouldn't have to read the book after all.

"Yes, there is."

He leaned back on a pillow, feeling more relaxed. That was fun, talking to a girl about schoolwork. A girl that he liked. "What question are you doing?"

"I'm not sure yet."

"Which one do you think I should do?"

Liz looked over the list for what she thought would be the easiest question and dictated it to him.

Brad was smiling as he copied it on the inside back cover of the book.

"Look," she said when she'd finished, "I've got to go."

"Okay. It was nice talking to you. I'll call tomorrow so you can tell me if I'm missing anything else. Thanks."

Liz hung up the phone and looked up at the ceiling. This is weird, she thought, this is very, very weird.

The next afternoon, while everyone else was filing out of math class, Liz went over to the window and opened it. "Come here, Terry," she called over her shoulder. "You won't believe this."

Terry walked over and looked out. "What? What is it?"

Liz opened the window a little more. "Breathe. It's warm. It's like spring."

Terry took a deep breath. She put her hand out the window. Water from melting snow dripped off the roof onto her palm. Bright blue sky, sunshine that warmed. "Heaven," Terry said.

Ben came up next to them and looked out the window. "What's up?"

"Spring," Liz said.

He put his hand out. "Spring? It's only March first. We had twelve inches of snow last April twentieth."

"Stop being so rational," Terry scolded. "Today it's spring." She turned to them. "Let's get Joey and go for ice cream cones at Sewards."

"Or better yet hot fudge sundaes." Liz's mouth watered when she said the words.

As they were rushing toward the lockers to find Joey, Liz whispered to Terry, "What'll I do about Dary?"

"Can't she walk home alone for once?"

"I have to at least invite her."

"What a drag."

Liz found Dary waiting for her in front of the school. Other kids, made happy by the break in the weather, were hanging around longer than usual.

"It's sunny," Liz said, "it's a beautiful day. Do you want to go for a walk?" It took some pantomime and more words, but finally Dary pretty much understood what Liz was asking.

"No," Dary said. "I go home one."

"Alone," Liz corrected. "Say 'I'll go home alone.' "

Dary obediently repeated it, then did it.

"Bye," Liz called after her. "See you tomorrow."

"You bet," Dary called back with a smile. "So long."

A few minutes later Liz, Ben, Joey, and Terry walked arm in arm, coats and jackets open, across the street in front of the school toward downtown and Sewards. Several times they had to break up to let other kids pass or for one or the other of them to hop a puddle. After a block of this they split into twos.

"Tell me now it isn't spring?" Liz teased Ben.

"It isn't," he said with a laugh.

"There were twelve inches of snow late last April," Joey reminded them.

"So we've heard," Liz said.

Terry groaned. "No more snow."

Joey put his arm around her. "Oh poor thing. She melts in the snow." He left his arm there.

Ben wanted to put his arm around Liz but knew in a few

90

minutes they'd be passing Lee's Chinese. He couldn't risk it. What if his father was looking out the window? "Come on," he said to her. "Let's catch up." He ran ahead to walk next to Joey.

Liz moved up next to Terry and said, "You want to go to the mall in Burlington with my mother and me on Saturday? We'll have lunch and look at spring clothes."

Terry was holding the hand that Joey had lightly placed on her shoulder. "Can't. I'm working at the hospital. I promised."

Sewards was jammed. "Guess we're not the only ones who have good ideas," Joey said. They walked by a group of juniors and seniors to the only available booth. Liz saw Alex Cranston looking her up and down.

"Hey Joey," Alex called out. "How's it going?"

Joey stopped in front of Alex's booth and put his arm around Terry again. "All right."

"How are you, Liz?" Alex asked with a wide, friendly grin.

"I'm all right too, Alex," she answered.

"Hey Ben," Alex said. "Hi."

"Hi," Ben answered.

"So, are you two an item?" Alex asked.

Liz felt her face flush. Ben, for the first time she could remember, was at a loss for words. He didn't answer Alex's question. Terry finally answered for them, "Sort of."

Alex repeated, "Sort of?" in a mocking, high-pitched imitation of Terry. The five kids in the booth with him laughed.

Liz pushed ahead of Terry and Joey and slid across the bright blue plastic seat to the far end of their booth. To cover her embarrassment she asked no one in particular, "Why does everyone have to be an item?"

"Alex is just jealous because he wanted to go out with you," Joey said as he moved into the booth and sat across from her.

"Besides, anyone who sees you two can tell you're sort of an item," Terry said as she pushed in next to Joey.

Ben sat next to Liz. "He did?" he asked her.

"Did what? Who?"

"Alex. Did he want to go out with you?" he asked again.

Liz picked up her menu. "Ask Joey. He seems to know all about it."

She opened the menu and scanned the list of items and prices even though she knew what she wanted.

"Our Lizzy is very popular with older men," Terry said.

Liz leaned over and hit her on the arm with the menu. "Stop it. You're embarrassing me." But she was glad that Ben found out that a hotshot like Alex wanted to go out with her. She smiled at Ben. "What are you going to have?"

Later, as Liz licked the last streak of fudge off her spoon, she saw Mrs. Dahm in her pink and white uniform, waiting on people at the soda fountain counter. Their eyes met and Liz smiled and waved with her free hand. Mrs. Dahm waved back. Liz wondered what Mrs. Dahm thought of her being with Ben.

When she was on her way to the bathroom Liz stopped at the counter to say hello to Mrs. Dahm. "Dary is learning very fast," she added.

"You very good teacher."

"Does she talk English at home?"

"You bet," Mrs. Dahm said, "with my children. I say all time to talk to Dary in English."

"That's good."

Liz pictured Dary with the two young Dahm boys alone in the apartment while her aunt and uncle worked long

hours. "I think Dary would like a pair of jeans," she said. She raised her leg to show Mrs. Dahm. "You know— dungarees. More like American kids."

"Yes. Like American," Mrs. Dahm said. The *ping* of a bell signaled her. "One minute please," she said to Liz as she turned to pick up the burger platter that the short-order cook slid through the opening from the kitchen.

"Maybe Dary could go shopping with me and my mother on Saturday. I could help her pick out American clothes."

"And study English?" Mrs. Dahm asked.

"Yes," Liz said. "That too."

"Mom," Liz told her mother at dinner that night, "I want to bring Dary shopping with us on Saturday. Okay?"

"What about Terry?"

"She's busy." Liz could tell that her mother didn't like the idea of bringing Dary along. "Dary needs some hip clothes, Mom. She doesn't even own a pair of jeans. Besides, she's never been to Burlington except maybe when her plane landed. It'll be fun to show her around."

Diane shot Tom a disappointed look.

"Won't it be a strain for you two to spend the whole day with someone who doesn't really speak English?" he asked.

"Look, I'll uninvite her if it's such a big deal," Liz said, annoyed at both of them.

"Sweetie, it's fine. I was just thinking it through," her mother answered. "You know what I'm worried about."

"What?" Liz challenged.

"That you'll spend so much time with Dary that you won't get your own schoolwork done."

"We're talking about a shopping trip, Mom, not a tutorial for the SATs."

They ate in silence.

Liz picked at her meatloaf. All she'd meant to do when she invited Dary was to have a good time and maybe do a kind thing. But her parents made it into such a big deal. And now she wondered whether her mother was right, if Dary would be a big drag on Saturday.

Finally Tom broke the tense mood. "Well, there were some changes on Main Street today."

"What happened?" Diane was grateful to her husband for bringing up a new subject.

"Old Pop Stangoni sold his fruit and vegetable market."

"I thought his son would take it over," Diane commented.

"Young Freddie's off to the big city. Wants to be a lawyer."

"So who bought it?"

"Some Koreans. Two brothers and their families—the Kwons. Stangoni brought them into the shoe store to introduce me."

"Koreans?" Diane looked doubtful. "Do you think they'll do as good a job as the Stangonis?"

"I don't know why not," Tom answered. "Once they learn the ropes."

"Two families. How many of them are there?"

"Three size eights, a size six, a size five and a half, a size five . . ." Liz and her mother smiled at one another as he continued, "a child's two, and a pair of booties."

"Are you saying that all eight people bought shoes, Dad?"

"No, but they will. I was just sizing them up with my eyes."

"I guess there'll be more kids at your school. More kids to learn English," Liz's mother added.

"They seemed to know at least a little English," her father continued. "I think one of the brothers has been in

94

the states for a year and the other one just came. Two of the kids looked like they might be high school age."

"Maybe they'll make friends with Dary," her mother said.

Elizabeth hoped they would. "Dary's Cambodian, Mom, not Korean. Koreans and Cambodians don't even speak the same language. Just because people are Asians doesn't mean they're going to be friends."

"Of course not. You're absolutely right," her mother replied. "Any more than just because people are Europeans they're friends. Like the Irish and Italians when they came to America." She smiled at her husband. "Right, Tom?"

Tom winked at his daughter. "Says one good Italian woman to one good Irish man."

"Come to think of it, your parents weren't exactly thrilled when you took up with me," her mother added.

He chuckled. "You know what I just remembered?"

"What?" Liz and her mom asked at the same time.

"How upset my father was when his friend, McDonough, sold the fruit and vegetable store to Pop Stangoni."

"Why?" Liz asked.

"Because Fred Stangoni wasn't Irish."

"You mean Grandpa really was prejudiced against the Italians?"

Her father nodded. "To him Italians were the foreigners. He figured he got here first. And the Italians were swarthy compared to the fair Irish. And their food smelled different."

"Well, your father never complained about the smell of my spaghetti sauce," Diane interjected.

"And they probably didn't know any English when they first came," Liz said.

"You got it," Tom answered. "But Mario Stangoni and I were in the same class and we became best friends." Liz remembered the photos in her father's class yearbook. Ma-

95

rio and Tom, cocaptains of the football team, smiling at one another instead of the camera. "Anyway," her father continued, "Mario's the one who introduced me to your mother." He smiled at his wife.

"That's sweet," Liz said. But she wasn't thinking of her mother's romance with her father. She was thinking of her romance with Ben.

Ben was thinking of Liz too. He sat across the dinner table from his mother. They were eating alone because his father and uncle were working late at the restaurant. Ben picked up a dumpling with his chopsticks. Neither of them had said anything for several minutes.

"It's sort of quiet without Rob," Ben told his mother before sticking the dumpling in his mouth.

She smiled. "Two years he's been in college. You just think of that idea now?"

"It's not the first time. I was just thinking about how much he talks at suppertime." What he was thinking was that he wished Rob were home to help him talk to his parents about Liz. His brother was always better than he was at convincing his parents that they should let them do the things their friends did. Like the time Ben had wanted to go on a camping trip. If Rob was home now Ben would tell him about Liz and then Rob would help him talk to his parents. On his own he didn't even know where to begin. The dumpling felt like a lump in his stomach.

"You know the girl who called me the other day?" he started.

"Science partner girl?" his mother asked.

"Her name is Elizabeth Gaynor. She's very smart."

"Not as smart as you," his mother said.

"I don't know about that. I'd say she's as smart. She's

good in English literature too. She really understands plot and character."

"You know many stories and you read lots of books. All the time."

"I know." This wasn't going the way he wanted it to. But he forged on. "Elizabeth is a nice girl. I like her."

"Is she the number one student?" his mother asked.

"I think we're both number one, Mom."

"Impossible two number one. You should study more." She stood to clear the table. "Eat your dinner."

As she went to the sink with the dishes, Tia Lee reflected that it was too bad there weren't Chinese students for her son to have as friends. Well, she'd make sure that he went to a college that was not only one of the best, but one where there would be many Chinese and he could have many Chinese friends. Then he'd find a nice Chinese girl to marry. In the meantime he needed to study hard and take advantage of the opportunities in America. She and her husband had had to settle for working in restaurants all of their lives, but their children could be anything. Especially if they went to the best colleges. She went back to the table, telling Ben for the ten thousandth time, "You are a Chinese boy. To do good in America you have to do better than American boy or girl. Much competition. No time for friends."

"Where was I born?" Ben asked.

His mother joked in Chinese, "You're not such a smart boy after all if you don't know where you were born." She continued in English, "You don't remember? Chicago."

"And Chicago is in America, right?" He was trying not to raise his voice.

"Of course."

"And what language do I speak?"

"English."

"So I'm American, Mom. Asian American."

"Not Asian American," his mother corrected. "Asian American is Koreans and Japanese and Vietnamese and all those low-class people. Maybe you're Chinese American. But Chinese first."

"Are we ever going back to China? Am I going to live there?"

His mother's eyes filled with tears. "No. For many years I hope yes, but now I know we never go back." She glared at her son. "And now I don't even have a Chinese son. Just another fresh American kid."

TEN

Terry ran up behind Liz and put her arm around her. "Hey, guess what?"

Liz jumped, startled.

"Sorry," Terry said. "I didn't mean to scare you."

"It's okay, I was looking at the display. What do you think?"

Standing side by side in front of the shoe store they studied Liz's spring window display. Two five-foot-high white Easter rabbits stood paw to paw. One was wearing black and white wing-tipped shoes and a top hat. The other was decked out in a pair of open-toed red high heels and a red straw hat with a veil. The rabbits' white and pink floppy ears stuck through slits that Liz had cut in the hats. There was a big straw laundry basket painted and decorated to look like an Easter basket. Instead of candy it was chock full of new shoes. Twenty more pairs were laid out in neat, even rows around the basket so that customers could see all the new styles.

"I like it," Terry said, "especially the way the fur sticks

through the holes on her shoes. Are you going to have a message, like 'Happy Spring' or something?"

"Maybe. I have to think about it. But it looks okay so far, don't you think?"

"I think it looks great."

The sun was going down behind the post office building so the chill of late winter moved in where the early spring sun had warmed the air just moments before. Liz shivered. "I better go in and clean up the mess I made in the back. Come with me."

"Can't. I've got to meet Joey. I'm already late."

"You have another date?"

"We're going to his brother's for dinner. It's his father's birthday." She held open her coat to show Liz her short dark blue dress with a red-and-white-checked scarf. "Do I look okay?"

"You look beautiful. But Terry, you're going to a family gathering? This is serious."

"It's no big deal."

Liz laughed. "Oh really?"

"Come on," Terry pleaded. "You're just teasing me. Anyway what I stopped by to tell you is that I can go shopping with you in Burlington tomorrow. I don't have to sub for Karen at the hospital after all. I mean if it's all right with your mother."

"Of course it'll be all right with my mother. Dary's coming too. I mean I invited her after you said you couldn't come." Liz folded her arms and moved closer to the building to get out of the wind's path. "My mother will be real glad you're coming. She wasn't so thrilled that I invited Dary, you know, because Dary doesn't know English that well."

"Dary doesn't know English at all, Liz. I mean, hardly at all. Anything she knows you taught her. And you'll spend the whole day teaching her more. Does she have to come?"

"I already invited her. To get some jeans."

"She can get jeans in Rutland."

"I can't uninvite her, Terry."

"What a drag. We won't be able to have a normal conversation. Look, Liz, I think it's great what you're doing for Dary and everything. But, you know, I do my volunteer work at the hospital. I'd like to just relax and not have to worry about anybody on the weekend. Know what I mean?" She put her arm around her friend. "Don't be hurt, but I don't want to go if Dary's going."

"So don't." Liz shrugged herself free of Terry's arm. "It's cold. I'm going in."

"Don't be mad. I'll talk to you tomorrow when you get back. Buy lots of gorgeous spring things."

"Sure," Liz said as she turned to go in. She was angry at Terry and angry at Dary. And angry at herself for being angry with Dary. What was wrong with everyone, anyway? It was just shopping.

"How about Sunday?" Terry called after her. "Come over to my place. We'll hang out."

"Can't," Liz said over her shoulder. "I have a date with Ben."

"You do? You didn't . . ."

Liz couldn't hear the rest because she'd already closed the door between herself and Terry.

An hour later, as Liz and her father were leaving the store, a voice from across the street shouted, "Mr. Gaynor." A Korean man was looking both ways for a break in the traffic so he could cross the road to meet them. "One minute, Mr. Gaynor," he called.

"You stay there, Mr. Kwon," Tom called back. "We'll come over."

While they waited for the light to change, Liz's father

explained what she'd already guessed. "That's Mr. Kwon. The Korean who bought Stangoni's store." Liz read the big red, white, and blue banner that was strung across the old STANGONI'S FRUITS AND VEGETABLES sign. UNDER NEW MANAGEMENT, it read. OPEN TWENTY-FOUR HOURS. Her father saw the sign too and wondered what the Chamber of Commerce would think about it.

In the familiar old-fashioned fruit and vegetable market Liz looked around at new faces. New Asian faces. She shook hands with all of them, including two teenagers— Soon-Je Kwon and Jae-Hyuk Kwon—who seemed to be around her age. "Nice to meet you," Liz said. She noticed that they were already dressed in American jeans and sweatshirts.

"Soon-Je and Jae-Hyuk go to school," Mr. Kwon told her. "I think this Ethan Allen High School is a good school. We want good school. Many opportunities for education in America."

"Yes," Liz said.

"Daughter know English some," Mr. Kwon explained. "But need much work. Nephew new to America. Need much, much work."

Liz smiled. One thing was for sure, she was not about to be their English teacher. But maybe Soon-Je could be Dary's friend. It would be such a relief to go back to hanging out with her old friends at school without having to worry about whether she was being understood whenever she opened her mouth.

A few minutes later Liz and her father found themselves holding bags of fruits and vegetables that Mr. Kwon insisted they take as a gesture of friendship.

"Bye," Liz said as she tried to wave without letting go of her bag.

Jae-Hyuk said, "Bye."

Soon-Je said, "See in school."

"Yes," Liz said. "I'll introduce you to some people."

By nine-thirty on Saturday morning, Liz and her mother and Dary were driving along Route 7A to Burlington. It was another "spring is in the air" March morning. "I'm taking this way instead of Route 7," her mother told Dary, "because it's a much prettier route. We'll pass farms this way. It'll take a little longer, but on a day like this it's worth it."

Dary smiled and nodded.

"Did she understand me?" Liz's mother asked.

"Probably not," Liz said. She leaned forward and stuck a tape in the tape deck. "Let's listen to music instead of talking."

"Fine with me," her mother said. "As long as it's not heavy metal."

Liz glanced at Dary's reflection in the rearview mirror. She seemed content to watch the passing scenery. Liz adjusted the speaker control so that the music wouldn't blast Dary out of the backseat.

An hour later they stood on Church Street in Burlington looking down the escalator that led into the underground shopping mall.

Dary looked apprehensive. "Stairs run," she said as she took a step back.

Liz realized that Dary had never seen an escalator before. "It's okay," Liz said. "No problem."

Dary stepped farther back.

"You go down the stairs," Liz said pointing to the set of regular stairs beside the escalator. "My mother and I will go on the escalator."

As they rode the escalator together, Diane said, "Isn't that adorable. She called the escalator 'stairs that run.' "

"She's got to learn the right words." Liz felt a little

resentful. She had just wanted to treat Dary to a shopping trip, but how could she relax if she had to worry about Dary all the time? She always had to be thinking, what does Dary know? What doesn't she know? What will frighten her?

Diane put her arm through her daughter's as they stepped off the escalator. "Cheer up. We'll have a good day. Let's make the best of it and help her get some good clothes. Okay?"

They watched Dary walking down the last few stairs. "What name stairs that run?" she asked them.

"Es-ca-la-tor," Diane answered. "Say it."

All the way to the Denim Dreams store Diane and Dary practiced "es-ca-la-tor," and Liz thought ruefully about how much more fun she could have been having with Terry.

The first two pairs of jeans that Dary tried on were too big. Finally Diane found a petite pair that fit just right. Liz tried on a denim miniskirt, a pair of shorts, and two short-sleeved cotton tops. Her mother said she could get all four pieces. Then she helped Dary pick out two brightly colored T-shirts which were as up-to-date as you could get without being exactly like the ones she'd picked out for herself.

Dary beamed at her own image in the mirror. "Jeans," she said.

"Very pretty," Diane told her.

"Beautiful," Liz added. "You should wear them home."

"You bet," Dary agreed.

When she'd paid up, Dary only had ten dollars left.

"I need something at the lingerie shop," Diane told them when they'd left Denim Dreams. "Why don't you show Dary around and I'll meet you both at Boves in about forty minutes?"

Liz led Dary around the corner to another underground street of storefronts. Dary was happily swinging her bag

and catching the reflection of her dungareed legs in the store windows. "Much fun," she told Liz. "Very American."

"And we'll have pizza for lunch," Liz said. "You know what pizza is."

"You bet," Dary said.

They walked along, Liz studying the stream of shoppers to see if she'd recognize anyone from Burlington High. Maybe someone she'd met at the statewide science fair or basketball games. Stopping in front of Miriam's Magic Boutique she said to Dary, "This store's neat. Let's go in." But Dary wasn't next to her.

I knew it, Liz thought, trying not to panic as she walked back in the direction she'd come from. I knew she'd get lost. She found Dary staring at the window display of Nu Nails by Lillian.

"Beautiful," Dary told Liz. She was pointing to a pair of mannequin hands with long painted fingernails. "Very beautiful." She held her ten dollars out to Liz. "I buy red. Must grow finger."

"Nails," Liz corrected. "Must grow fingernails." She touched the small nail on Dary's index finger. "Nails grow on fingers." She pointed to her feet. "Nails grow on toes." She held out a strand of her own hair. "Hair grows on the head."

After they'd sat down for lunch at Boves and ordered a meatball pizza, Dary laid out her nail products on the table. Diane looked them over: nail strengthener, emery boards, red polish, cover polish, remover, and a bag of cotton balls and swabs. "All this for ten dollars?" Diane asked.

Liz laughed. "No way. Lillian liked Dary so she gave her all this stuff. She told me that Cambodian women love to have long nails. She said Dary's nails had been malnourished, but that except for one nail, the new nails coming in would be strong. Lillian knows a lot about fingernails."

Dary held out the index finger of her left hand. "Not so good," she said. "But it grow. I eat." The waiter placed the large pizza in front of them and they each took a slice.

"I eat milk food too," Dary said. "Grow strong."

Oh no, Liz thought, I forgot about the cheese on pizza. "Maybe you should take it off," Liz said. She demonstrated by lifting a piece of cheese off Dary's slice and replacing it with the meatball from her own slice. "You take my meat, I'll take your cheese. That way you won't get sick."

"Okay," Dary agreed.

It was Diane's idea that when they got back to Rutland that afternoon they stop at the shoe store and get Dary a pair of sneakers to go with her new clothes.

When they'd finally dropped Dary and her packages off at the Dahm apartment Liz told her mother, "You were really nice to her. Thank you."

"Well, it was the least I could do. It's so clear she's had a horrible, horrible time."

"Mom, she must have such terrible memories. Her whole family was probably wiped out when she was just this little kid. And how on earth did she get herself to a border camp in Thailand without being killed?"

Diane sighed. "We can't even imagine what she went through, can we?"

ELEVEN

"Hi."

"Hi. Come on in."

Ben stepped into the front hall and closed the door behind him. Liz is so pretty, he thought. I love the way her hair hangs down around her face like that.

"We can go right downstairs," Liz said, brushing her hair behind her ears, "unless you want a soda or something first."

"No thanks." As he followed her down the stairs to the family room he told her, "I saw the Easter window you did for your store. It looks great."

At the bottom stair she turned toward him. "Thanks."

Ben stood one step above her and looked down at the top of her head. This is what it would be like to be a guy who's six-feet-two instead of five-feet-nine, he thought. He took the last step and faced her at a more equal height and decided he liked it better this way. He kissed her on the lips.

"Hi again," he said after the kiss.

They held hands walking over to the television set. "I already set up the videotape," she told him. "I watched it with my mother last year. It pretty much follows the book."

"Do you think we'll find enough differences between the book and the movie for the essay question?" Ben asked. He sat down on the couch.

"It'll be easy. We can talk about how they use camera angles and close-ups to focus your attention. Stuff like that." Liz picked up the remote controls for the television and the VCR and sat down next to Ben on the couch. "We can stop the tape whenever we have an idea."

Ben took out a pad and a pencil. I don't care about this movie or this homework, he thought. I care about Liz. I love being close to her.

He kissed me and we're together on this couch, Liz thought. There's no way we're going to get much work done.

She turned on the TV and pressed the play button on the VCR remote control. Ben put his arm over the top of the couch. She laid her head back on his arm. They stayed like that through the first few scenes of the movie. When two of the main characters danced together for the first time at the ball, it reminded Liz of the first time she'd danced with Ben. She said, "You're a good dancer. I liked dancing with you at the Valentine's Day dance."

"You too. I liked dancing with you. Until Brad cut in."

"Yeah, I know what you mean. And he won't give up, either. Since he's been suspended he's calling me all the time to get the schoolwork he's missing."

Ben took the remote control out of her hand and turned off the movie. "Calling you?" he said. "Like every day?"

Liz nodded.

"Why you? Why doesn't he call someone else? And what's this about homework? He never does his work. He doesn't

even know what's going on in the classes." Ben continued, "I hate having guys like that in our classes. They hold everybody back."

Liz shifted onto the other couch cushion and faced him. She didn't like the turn the conversation had taken. Ben sounded so superior. "Brad might be slow in schoolwork and a pain sometimes," she said, "but he's got as much right to an education as you or I do." To her surprise she heard real anger in her voice.

"He's not getting an education," Ben said in an even, calm voice. "He's just filling a seat and making trouble. Why are you defending him?" He felt disappointed in Liz. Did she go for all that macho stuff—tall men with overdeveloped muscles, pickup trucks, and a "don't mess with me" attitude.

"Are we having a fight?" Liz asked.

"No, it's a discussion." He studied the red and blue markings on the remote control panel.

"What are you thinking?" she asked.

"That maybe you really like Brad."

"You mean like him like a guy?" Liz remembered the closeness she'd felt with Ben just minutes before. How could he think she liked Brad that way? "Of course I don't. I just feel a little sorry for him sometimes. Brad's always putting his big foot in his mouth."

"His big racist foot in his big racist mouth. Have you heard some of the things he's called me?"

"I'm sorry. You're right. I wasn't remembering that."

"Well I remember it. I can't just shrug off comments like that. And that whole thing with his flat tire? And look how he's frightened Dary Sing. I'm surprised you forgot about that so quickly."

Liz thought about Dary and how Brad just driving by in his truck made her uneasy. And how Dary seemed to make

Ben uneasy. She was surprised that Ben had even mentioned Dary. "Why don't you like her?" she asked.

"Dary?"

"Yes, Dary. You don't seem to like her. You wouldn't help her that first day. You avoid me when I'm with her. I wonder why."

"I don't dislike her. I guess I'm just not interested in her." He moved closer to Liz. "You're the one I'm interested in." He stared at her, trying to read her expression. "Are you mad at me?" he asked.

"No. I'm just confused. I think there's more to what's going on between you and Dary than you're admitting."

"You mean like I'm avoiding her because I really like her? That's crazy!"

"I thought that at first. But I don't anymore. I just think you've been pretty weird around her and I wonder why."

"That's how I feel about you and Brad," he said.

They heard the front door open and close. "Who's that?" Ben asked.

"My mother doesn't get out of work until later. It must be my father."

They moved apart. Each sat on their own couch cushion.

Liz pushed the play button and the actors resumed their dance around the ballroom floor. "Hi, kids," her father yelled from the top of the stairs.

"Hi, Dad."

"Hello, Mr. Gaynor."

He came bounding down the stairs. "How's it going?"

"Okay," Liz answered. "We just got started."

"Well, don't let me interrupt you." He stood next to the couch and watched the TV screen. "I remember this movie. Your mother loves it."

"Yeah," Liz answered. "We're comparing the movie and the book for English class."

Her father shifted nervously from one foot to another. He looked a little agitated. Was he upset that she was alone down there with a boyfriend?

"Dad," she said, stopping the film, "is something wrong? You seem sort of fidgety."

"We just had an emergency meeting of the Chamber of Commerce," he said. "Your father was there too, Ben. It was disturbing. There hasn't been this much dissension among the downtown merchants in years. Everyone was so emotional."

"What about?"

"The new owners of Stangoni's market."

"The Kwons?" Liz asked. "What's the problem?"

"I really shouldn't talk about it. I'm sorry I interrupted. Go back to your movie." He patted Liz affectionately on the head and went back up the stairs thinking that *Pride and Prejudice* couldn't have been a more apt title for the meeting he'd just gone to.

"I didn't know Stangoni sold the market," Ben said.

"I met the new owners," Liz said. "Two brothers and their families. They're Korean." She smiled to herself remembering how her father knew all their shoe sizes. "A couple of the kids are in high school."

"Great." He said it sarcastically. "That's just great."

"Why does it bother you that they've moved here?"

"Look, I wouldn't mind who moved here if people had enough brains to tell the difference between me and those fresh-off-the-boat people."

"But that's prejudiced."

"Prejudiced? What's prejudiced is when jerks like Brad think I'm just another chink who's part of the Asian invasion."

Liz was too surprised and confused by Ben's outburst to argue with him.

Ben punched the movie back on and neither of them mentioned Brad, Dary, or the Koreans for the rest of the afternoon. They didn't kiss or hold hands again either.

That night while Liz was washing her hair in the shower she remembered the easy closeness with Ben followed by their argument. She didn't know which annoyed her more: Ben's prejudice against people like Brad whom he labeled "without enough brains" or his prejudice against people like the Kwons whom he called "fresh-off-the-boat people." And how could Ben think she felt about Brad the way she *had* felt about him. She stepped out of the shower and wrapped herself in a red-and-yellow-checked beach towel. How could Ben think I would like a jerk like Brad? she wondered. She wiped the steam off the mirror with the end of the towel and said out loud to her reflection, "You're doing it too."

Later, lying in bed, she thought over her feelings toward Ben and how their friendship had grown over the year and a half she had known him. And how in a few short weeks that friendship had developed into a romance. Now, in one afternoon, the romance seemed to have evaporated. Had the friendship evaporated too? Did she understand Ben Lee at all? Maybe they wouldn't even go back to being like they were before the romance. She already missed him.

Dary was in her seat when Liz walked into the classroom Monday morning. Liz noticed that she sat as primly as ever even though she was dressed in her new jeans, a bright pink shirt, and sneakers. She smiled up at Liz and handed her an envelope. "For shoes," she said.

Liz said, "No. The shoes were a present. A gift from my mother."

"Aunt say pay," Dary said. "She work. Have money."

I won't argue with her now, Liz thought. She took the envelope.

"Hey," Terry yelled to Liz as she walked toward her. "Dary's clothes are terrific."

When Ben came in he too went right over to Liz. "Here," he said, handing her some papers. "I photocopied the notes from our work yesterday."

The bell rang. Ben moved off to his own place in the back of the room. Terry whispered to Liz, "You did homework on your date?"

"I think that's all it's going to be," Liz said. She stuck the papers in her notebook and sat down. "I'll tell you about it later."

"Too bad," Terry said sympathetically.

Mr. Madison didn't come into the room until after homeroom announcements. When he did he was accompanied by Jae-Hyuk and Soon-Je Kwon.

"Settle down, class," Mr. Madison called out. He sounded cranky when he added, "Now."

Brad came in, brushing past the two new students and Mr. Madison. "I'm on time," he declared loudly. "I was in the dean's office getting unsuspended." He held out a few sheets of wrinkled paper. "Look. I did my work from last week when I wasn't here."

"Excuse me, Mr. Mulville," Mr. Madison said. "That's not what we're doing here right now. Just take your seat and we'll deal with all that in a minute."

"Hey, man," Brad mumbled as he turned away and headed toward his seat. "I'm just doing my work." He grumbled as he headed up the aisle, "Everybody's against me." He gave Ben a quick jab on the arm. "I haven't forgotten that you messed me up, man."

"Class," Mr. Madison said. "I'd like to introduce Jae-Hyuk Kwon and Soon-Je Kwon. They're new students to our school and have been assigned to our homeroom."

Jae-Hyuk Kwon and Soon-Je Kwon bowed slightly. A

chorus of halfhearted his, hellos, and welcomes sputtered through the room.

"Hello," Jae-Hyuk and Soon-Je answered with shy smiles as they looked over the new faces. Soon-Je spotted Liz and made a little wave. "Hello, Liz."

Everyone turned to look at Liz. "Hi," she answered back.

"You already know our new students?" Mr. Madison asked Liz.

"Their store is across the street from my father's," Liz explained. "I just met them."

"Do they speak English?" Edward called out.

"A little," Mr. Madison answered. "And I need a volunteer to show them around. To introduce them to their teachers and show them the ropes." He looked at Ben. "I suppose you don't speak Korean either?"

"No sir," Ben answered. "I don't."

"So," Mr. Madison continued to the whole class, "do I have any volunteers?"

Silence.

Liz could see that Jae-Hyuk and Soon-Je were embarrassed to be just standing there, waiting.

"How about Liz?" someone called out.

Mr. Madison and the whole class looked at her again. "I . . . ah . . . I'm very busy with Dary Sing," she told them. "She still needs a lot of help."

"Of course," Mr. Madison agreed. "You've got your hands full and you've been doing a splendid job. One more call for a volunteer."

Mr. Madison fiddled with some papers on his desk, trying to hide his embarrassment. When no one spoke up, he looked up and smiled at Jae-Hyuk and Soon-Je and said, "I'll get someone from my second-period class to help you." Ben noticed how Mr. Madison glared at the class and thought, he's probably going to take this out on us by marking our term projects really hard.

114

"I'll need two desks from Room 209," Mr. Madison continued. "Joey and Brad, do you think you could manage that much?"

"Glad to, Mr. Madison," Joey said.

Then Brad stood up. "Listen, Mr. Madison, I'll show those new guys around too. I'll take care of them."

Mr. Madison considered the offer for a second, then smiled. "All right Brad. Thank you."

Amazed at Brad's offer everyone, including Liz, turned to look at him. "I'll do it for service credit," Brad added. He winked at Liz, then left the room with Joey to get the extra desks.

"Brad'll be a big help," someone called out. "He'll show them how to cut classes."

"And how to fail," another added. There were some titters.

"Enough," Mr. Madison shouted. "This is not the easiest situation and I'd like a little cooperation. So just settle down. Take out your vocabulary books and review for tomorrow's quiz."

While the class did as they were directed, Mr. Madison looked at Jae-Hyuk and Soon-Je and sighed. "Let's see what we can do to help you. Do you know the English alphabet?" He wrote an *A* and *B* on his pad and showed them.

"Alphabet," Soon-Je said. "Yes and I know how to sound out words. I live in America one year already."

"Terrific," Mr. Madison said. He handed her a vocabulary book. "You just try to follow along with the rest of us for now. What about Jae-Hyuk?"

"He just come. Must learn English."

"Well, you will help him. Third period you'll meet with your special English teacher."

"Okay," Soon-Je told Mr. Madison before speaking softly in Korean to her cousin.

Brad was pushing a desk into the room. I bet Liz is really impressed that I'm the only one who volunteered to show them around, he thought. I'll get her to tell me what to do. "Move back, so I can have one on each side of me," he commanded Ben.

As Ben moved his desk he could feel his stomach tense up. The back of this room is going to turn into a circus, he thought.

Jae-Hyuk and Soon-Je, carrying their brand-new three-ring notebooks and pencil cases, walked to the back corner.

"Brad," Brad said to them as he pointed to himself. He proudly gestured to the two seats. "You sit." Then he sat down. "I sit."

Only one person got a snicker out before Mr. Madison scanned the room with a look that said, *Don't you dare laugh.*

"We got ourselves a little Chinatown back here," Brad proudly announced to the class.

"They're not Chinese," Ben said in an angry voice. "They're Korean."

"You all look alike to me," Brad said.

"Well, we're not all alike," Ben answered sharply.

"Brad!" Mr. Madison yelled out.

"What'd I say wrong?" Brad asked. "I just thought, I mean, the skin's the same. And their eyes are all sort of slanty. Man, if he says they're different then they're different. Nobody told me that." He pointed to Jae-Hyuk and Soon-Je. "So, they come from Korea." He pointed to Dary. "Where's she from?"

"Dary Sing was born in Cambodia," Mr. Madison said patiently.

"And you?" Brad pointed to Ben. "China, right?"

"Wrong," Ben said. "I come from Chicago." Ben was shoving his books and papers back into his bookbag. "I'm an American, you idiot, just like you."

Everyone, including Mr. Madison, was shocked and speechless as Ben made a quick exit out the back door of the room.

Brad was the first to speak. "I don't get it," he said. "He looks Chinese to me."

Liz was wondering if she should go after Ben when Joey stood up and asked, "Can I go look for him?"

Mr. Madison said, "Yes, please."

David, who sat next to Joey, raised his hand and suggested, "Maybe I should change places with Ben?"

"Thank you, David," Mr. Madison said. "Go ahead, Joey." He looked at his two new students. "Jae-Hyuk and Soon-Je, I'm sorry for the disruption, the . . ." he waved his hands around to try to indicate what he meant, "the mess. Our school is not like this."

"Is okay," Soon-Je said. "I go to big school in New York City. Sometime much trouble." She smiled and everyone smiled with her. And then the class got down to work.

Liz opened her vocabulary book, but she couldn't concentrate on her work. Her ears still rang with Ben's angry words. She pictured how he looked in the back of the room with Brad and the new Korean students. She remembered what Ben had said the day before about not wanting to be clumped together with the new immigrants. She'd never seen Ben so riled up—about anything. And Brad. What on earth was he doing volunteering to help the new students when he couldn't even get himself through the school day? It's because of me, she realized. Brad is helping Soon-Je and Jae-Hyuk to impress me. But why would he do that if he's so prejudiced against Asians? she wondered. Then it came to her in a flash. Brad wasn't prejudiced against Ben just because he was Asian. He was prejudiced against him because Ben was interested in her. She was caught in a lover's

triangle. She sat there staring blankly at the page of her vocabulary book. What a mess.

A few minutes later Joey came back in, whispered something to Mr. Madison, and took his place. When the bell finally signaled the end of the class, Liz, Terry, and Joey met in the hall.

"Did you find him?" Liz asked.

"Yeah. He was in the library. He'll go to his next class."

"I can't believe he ran out like that," Terry said. "It was like he was ashamed of being Chinese."

Liz said, "I don't think he's ashamed. I think he's angry."

"What'd he say?" Terry asked Joey. "Did he tell you why he did it?"

"Not really. He just said that Brad ruined everything. And that people like Brad are so narrow-minded and stupid that they make trouble for people like him."

They continued talking as they walked to their next class. "Why do you think Brad offered to help those Korean kids?" Terry asked. "It's not the sort of thing he does."

"I think that's part of what's upsetting Ben," Joey said. "He probably thinks Brad is doing it to get to him. But that doesn't make much sense."

"Why do you think Brad's doing it?" Terry asked Liz.

Liz had her own explanation for Brad's behavior. She knew that it didn't have as much to do with Ben as it did with her, but she shrugged her shoulders and told Joey and Terry, "Maybe Brad feels sorry for them."

TWELVE

Liz noticed Dary waiting for her next to the swinging doors leading to the cafeteria. *I don't want to have lunch with her today,* Liz thought. *I want to eat with my old friends. I need to talk to Ben.*

Dary was smiling as Liz came over. "How's it going?" Dary asked.

"Okay," Liz answered with a laugh. "Who taught you that, 'How's it going?' "

"In gym." They each took an orange plastic tray and moved along with the cafeteria line. "New girl and boy in English," Dary told Liz.

"Good," Liz said. She waved to Jae-Hyuk and Soon-Je, who were already coming off the line with their trays of food. Brad was leading them to a big table. When Dary saw them she screwed up her facial muscles into a scowl.

"What?" Liz asked.

"Brad bad?" Dary asked.

Liz felt like saying, *he's nothing but trouble.* Instead she answered, "He's being good to Jae and Soon." Liz still wondered what Brad had said or done to scare Dary.

Liz took a plate of tuna salad from the glass shelf. Dary took a tuna salad too. "To grow nails," she explained to Liz.

"Why don't you eat with Jae and Soon?" Liz asked her. "And make new friends."

"We save two place for you. Brad say, come now," Soon-Je said as she came over to them smiling.

Dary looked at Liz. "Okay?"

If I sit with them this time, Liz thought, maybe the next time Dary will sit with them by herself. "Okay," she agreed. As she followed Soon-Je to the table she looked around the cafeteria. Terry, Joey, and Ben were at a table with David and a couple of other kids from their class. She knew they were watching as she joined two Koreans, one Cambodian, and one big troublemaker for lunch.

Brad pulled out the empty chair next to him. "Have a seat."

Liz put her tray down and sat. "I've only got a few minutes for lunch," she told Brad. "I've got something to do in the science lab." There is no way I'm spending the entire lunch period sitting with all of you, Liz thought. I'll take Dary with me if I have to.

Brad smiled at her again. "How's the salad?"

"Okay." She saw that Dary was eating her salad too. Soon-Je was taking a bite out of an English muffin pizza and Jae-Hyuk was about to take a gulp of milk. "Wait," Liz told him. "Are you sure you can drink that?"

Startled by the urgency in her voice, Jae-Hyuk put the carton down and stared at it.

Liz turned to Soon-Je. "Can he drink it? Is milk okay?"

Soon-Je picked up the carton and sniffed through the opening. "Smell okay."

"But can he drink milk?" Liz asked.

Brad was smelling his milk. "Mine's okay."

"Yes," Soon-Je said. "Jae drink milk all the time."

Liz laughed and then explained about Dary. "I'm sorry." She smiled and nodded at Jae-Hyuk, who after his cousin said something to him in Korean hesitantly drank from the carton of milk.

As they ate in silence Liz couldn't help thinking that it seemed that she and Brad were their parents.

"I think I'm doing okay with this," Brad told her. "I bring them to the class and then meet them after." He took another gulp of his milk. "What else do you do with yours?"

"I teach Dary words," Liz said. "How to say them and spell them."

"Show me how you teach her words," Brad said. "I want to do this right."

He seems so sincere, Liz thought. Could this be the same Brad? He's sitting with these new kids in front of everyone. He can't be doing this just to impress me.

"So show me," Brad repeated.

"Okay," Liz said. She turned to Dary and gently tapped the table and asked, "What is this?"

"Table," Dary answered.

Liz nodded to Jae-Hyuk. Jae-Hyuk rubbed the top of the table and repeated, "Table."

Dary took out her notebook and showed Jae-Hyuk and Soon-Je the pages of drawings and labels that she'd done with Liz.

"Good," Soon-Je told Dary. "Very good. So many words for just learning English."

Dary smiled at Soon-Je. "Liz help me," she said. "All clock."

"All the time," Liz corrected. And they all laughed.

A few minutes later Liz told Dary, "I'm going to work in the science room. You stay here. Okay?"

Dary didn't answer with an okay, but suddenly looked apprehensive.

Brad included the others when he said, "Liz stay. Okay?"

They all smiled and said, "Stay. Stay."

"Sh-h-h. Okay. I'll stay," Liz said.

"Hey." David nudged Ben with his elbow. "What's with you and Brad? I've never seen you angry like that. I'd stay out of Brad's way. Unless you want a fistfight."

"Maybe you should, Ben," Joey agreed. "Fighting is the one thing Brad knows how to do. The guy's working toward a Rambo-sized body."

Ben shook his head and looked at his friends. "A Rambo-sized body with a pea-sized brain."

When the bell rang Terry whispered to Ben, "Maybe you should wait a minute. Let Brad go first. Might as well avoid trouble."

"Do you think I'm afraid of Brad?"

"No. But I think you should be."

A minute later Ben was walking down the hall behind Brad, Soon-Je, and Jae-Hyuk. Brad was speaking slowly and loudly. "Go to gym class. To play ball." Brad mimicked a jumpshot. "Ball games. Play."

Soon-Je spoke softly in Korean to her cousin, who smiled at Brad and said, "Okay."

They stopped in front of the gym doors. Ben watched and waited.

"So you"—Brad pointed at Soon-Je and Jae-Hyuk—"go to gym class. I"—he pointed at himself—"go to history class. After I be back here." He pointed to the spot where they stood. "Wait here. Okay?"

"Terrific," Soon-Je answered. "We meet you here after gym class."

"Good. Very good," Brad told her. "Good student."

122

As Soon-Je and Jae-Hyuk went through the swinging doors Brad turned to see Ben watching him. "What are you looking at?"

"You don't really have to talk to them like that."

"They're my friends. I'll talk to them how I want."

"They're as old as you are and probably a lot smarter so don't talk to them like they're babies."

"I'm teaching them English. What are you teaching them? You're the hotshot from Chicago. You don't even know their language."

"Maybe I'll teach them to stay away from racist jerks like you."

Brad moved closer to Ben. "Why is it you're always calling me a jerk? Why are you always insulting me like that? You're the one who's dumb, because I'm going to make you mush. You might have a fancy explanation for how a fist can make mush of a body, but it's your body that's going to be mush. Remember that." Brad shook his head. "Why do you keep bugging me?"

Ben heard his own voice, loud and sharp as he went on the verbal attack. "You're never up to any good so I just wonder what you're up to now. First you call me every insulting racist slur your pea-sized brain can come up with and now you're playing teacher/nursemaid to these new Korean kids. I don't get it. You going to call them yellow skin and slant-eyes too?"

"You better watch who you call pea brain or I'm going to wipe up this floor with your yellow brain." Every muscle in Brad's body was tensing for a fight.

Before Ben could answer, Joey was on one side of him, David on the other. "Let's get to class," Joey said.

"You coming or what?" David asked Ben.

Brad watched the three of them walk away from him toward the science lab and thought, why's that chink al-

ways putting me down? Why's he always messing with my business? First Liz. Now these new Korean kids. Why doesn't he mind his own business? Why doesn't he leave me alone?

"Thanks for the notes from yesterday," Liz said as she sat down next to Ben in science lab.

He continued setting up the Bunsen burner for the experiment and she noticed that he didn't even look up at her when he replied curtly, "You're welcome."

"You can borrow it," she added, wishing he'd look at her.

He looked up. "Borrow what?"

She studied his face, trying to see if there were any clues as to what he was thinking. She wondered if Terry was right when she said that Ben was ashamed of being Chinese. She wondered if it bothered Ben that he looked different from everyone else.

"Liz," he asked, "what are you staring at?" His voice sounded gentle now. "What are you saying I can borrow?"

"The videotape of *Pride and Prejudice*," she explained. "If you need to look at it again to do your paper. I mean, you don't have to come over to my house again. You could borrow it."

"I'll just rent it at the video store," Ben said. "Thanks anyway." He tightened the knob on the burner and kept his eyes down. I made a total fool of myself this morning, he thought. She's fed up with me. She doesn't even want me at her house again. Maybe it's best. I thought we had something going, but being with me isn't what she's used to, I guess. Maybe she really prefers someone like Brad. Someone she's known all her life. A real American.

Liz quickly walked to the supply closet in the back of the room so Ben wouldn't see the tears welling up in her eyes. What happened? she wondered. I guess it really is over,

and it never even had a chance. But why? Sure Ben and I are different, but we also have a lot in common. We're both smart and we want more than what our parents want for us. Parents—they shouldn't make a difference in our feelings for one another. Or was the big problem Ben? Maybe his own difficulties with being Chinese were coming between them. Why couldn't they talk about it?

During science Liz received a note asking her to report to Room 209A at the end of the day to see the special English teacher who came over from the junior high to teach Dary English. Liz wondered if she was going to be asked to help Soon-Je and Jae-Hyuk with their English too. She'd just say no. There was just so much anyone could expect her to do.

Ms. Stranton sat at one of five desks set up in a circle in Room 209A. It wasn't a regular classroom, but an old book room, just the right size for five or six people to have a meeting or sit around learning.

"Come in, Elizabeth." Ms. Stranton stood up with a welcoming smile. "Sit down." She offered Liz some nuts and raisins from a plastic bag.

"No thanks."

"You've been wonderful with Dary," Ms. Stranton said as she put the half-finished bag of trail mix away. "She's making amazing progress."

"Thank you."

"I was wondering how much of your time it takes to work with her like that."

Liz thought of the word-walks to and from school, the word-lunches, the word-weekend lesson, the word-shopping trip. "It does take up a lot of my time," she told Ms. Stranton.

"Does that interfere with your own schoolwork?"

"I don't think so. I mean, a lot of the time I'm with Dary

is time I'd be doing something else besides schoolwork, like being with my friends."

"I see." Ms. Stranton swung one leg over the other and watched her own foot swing to and fro. "I understand that you know Soon-Je and Jae-Hyuk Kwon?"

Please, Liz prayed, please don't ask me to help them too. "I met them because their store is across from our store," Liz explained. "Brad Mulville is helping them."

"So I noticed. I remember Brad from junior high. This isn't the sort of thing you'd think Brad would do, is it? I normally think of Brad as the student who needs extra help."

"I guess so." Liz found herself picking at her middle fingernail with her thumbnail and wondering, is she going to ask me to help Brad help Soon-Je and Jae-Hyuk? "I have to go pretty soon," she told Ms. Stranton.

Ms. Stranton uncrossed her legs and straightened up. "What I wanted to say, Liz, is that the principal and I have been looking over the situation here with our three new Asian American students in the high school. In addition to these three I have seven students at the junior high who are learning English. Two of them are from the Kwon family. Even though Dary, Jae-Hyuk, and Soon-Je are high school age, we're considering moving them into the junior high so that they can have more language work with me. Instead of splitting myself up between the two schools, I could have all ten students for half a day of special language classes and use the rest of the time helping them with the classes they attend with the regular student body."

"So Dary and Soon-Je and Jae-Hyuk would be put into junior high classes?"

"That's right. Socially, I'll admit, it's not the best idea. But since there's only one of me and now ten of them, we've been considering it. You've been so involved with

126

Dary I thought I'd ask you what you thought of that idea. Your teachers are also concerned that your work with Dary might be a burden for you. Perhaps we have depended on you too much."

"Well, working with Dary takes time," Liz told Ms. Stranton. At least, she thought, she's not asking me to do more. But did one of her teachers think she was slipping behind in her work? Was she?

"Anyway, Liz," Ms. Stranton said as she stood up, "I would like you to think about it for a couple of days. We won't make a decision until Friday. There's a lot to consider here. I just would like to know what you think. You're so close to Dary. Her only friend here, really. I'm concerned about how moving over to junior high might affect her progress in adjusting to America. So your opinion will count greatly."

"Dary must have had a terrible time before coming here," Liz commented. "Could you tell me what happened to her in Cambodia?"

"The files are pretty scant on that matter," Ms. Stranton said. "In any case I'm not at liberty to say what happened to her. Perhaps someday she will tell you herself."

"If she ever learns enough English."

"*When*," Ms. Stranton corrected. "When she learns enough English. You've done a great job with Dary, Elizabeth. Not just the English you've taught her, but by the way you've been her friend."

Dary was standing at the bottom step waiting for Liz when she came out of school.

"Hi, Liz," Dary called.

"Hi."

"Why sad?" Dary asked as they started walking. "Ben no boyfriend?"

127

How'd she figure that out? Liz wondered.

Dary's beautiful almond-shaped eyes shined with concern. "Sorry sad," she told Liz. "No worry. Be better."

As they started down the hill Liz said, "No words today. Okay?"

"Okay," Dary answered.

When Elizabeth went into her father's store one of the salespeople was straightening up a table display in the middle of the store. "Hi, Elizabeth," Louise said as she placed a pair of tiny pink baby sneakers next to a blue pair of the same size. "We're getting lots of compliments on your window."

"Great."

"Your father said you're adding a sign to it. What's it going to say?"

Liz grinned. "It's a surprise. I'm putting it up now, so you won't have to wait too long." As Liz opened her bag and pulled out a manila envelope of cutout letters she asked, "Where's my dad?"

"In the back. With Mr. Hadley."

"Mr. Hadley from the hardware store?"

Louise nodded. "And Marian Parenti."

Liz put down the envelope. "The pharmacist? How come?"

"Chamber of Commerce business. Things are all stirred up on Main Street since the Koreans took over Stangoni's."

Liz took off her coat and stepped up into the display window. She was laying out her letters on the floor space in front of the two stuffed rabbits when Mr. Hadley and Mrs. Parenti came out of the store onto the street and stood in front of the window. They were too engrossed in their conversation to notice her in the window display. She stayed perfectly still so she could hear what they said through the thick glass of the window.

"It'll ruin the town and our businesses," Mr. Hadley said.

"I still don't see why you think that," Marian Parenti answered.

"Marian, just look at that sign. 'Open twenty-four hours,' " Mr. Hadley said, pointing across the street. "You think they're just going to sell tomatoes and oranges? They'll be having all sorts of things stuffed on those shelves. Aspirin. Toothpaste. You'll suffer, Marian," Mr. Hadley admonished as they separated to go back to their own stores. "Mark my words."

After straining to hear Mr. Hadley and Mrs. Parenti talking on the street, Liz was startled when she heard her father's booming voice, "Hey, honey, how's it going in there?" As Liz turned toward her father's voice she collided with Mrs. Bunny and let out a yelp. Tom Gaynor poked his head into the display from the other side of Mr. Bunny. "You okay? Did it hurt you?"

Liz looked at her father over a mound of stuffed fake fur. "No. It just surprised me."

"I need some air," her father said. "Why don't you come over to Sewards with me?"

"What about my letters?" Liz asked as she righted Mrs. Bunny and straightened her Easter bonnet.

"Just leave them. You can do it later. Or tomorrow."

"I'll go with you to Sewards," she told her father.

"So how was your day?" Tom asked his daughter. He took a deep breath. The fresh air felt and smelled good to him after the leathery closeness of his back office and the tension of meeting with Hadley and Parenti.

"My day was okay. What about yours? I hear Mr. Hadley is really upset." She nodded in the direction of the new Korean market. "Why's everyone so upset about that store?"

"That's a good question." Her father was thoughtful for a

129

second. "They think they know what's bothering them, but I'm not quite sure that what they say is really what it's all about."

They walked past the economy clothing store and the pharmacy. Another half block and they'd be at Sewards.

"What do they think is bothering them?" Liz asked.

"That the market will be open twenty-four hours, seven days a week. The rest of us have a Monday-through-Saturday, nine-to-six schedule, with some of us staying open Thursday night. Parenti's Pharmacy is open for a few hours on Sunday. But that's about it for downtown. Hadley and some of the others think a twenty-four-hour store will invite a bad element. People who are partying or staying up all night will come downtown, folks from other towns."

"To buy fruits and vegetables? People don't usually end a wild night with fruit salad."

Her father opened the door for her. "What they're afraid of is that the Kwon family will sell other things—like beer, soda, crackers, paper products—and be more like a small general grocery than a fruit and vegetable market. Which of course will take business from the rest of the merchants or force them to keep longer hours than they want to."

"Has anyone asked them to sell only fruits and vegetables, like the Stangoni's did?" Liz asked as they sat in a booth up front. "And not to have such long hours?"

"We tried. At that meeting yesterday. Mr. Kwon said that he has a big family and has borrowed a lot of money to open the store. The only way he can see them making a go of it is by doing what his cousins in New York City are doing."

Liz completed the sentence. "Which is staying open twenty-four hours a day and selling lots of different things."

"Right."

They each ordered a chocolate ice cream soda.

"So what's going to happen now?" Liz asked.

"The Chamber of Commerce can take action. A lot of things could happen."

"But there's always been new people coming to town," Liz said. "Maybe the Kwons should try to fit in and not try something new right away like that."

Their sodas came and Tom took a long slurp before saying, "Well, maybe you're right. But Mr. Kwon isn't handling it that way. Probably because of the language problem and cultural differences. I'm not even sure he understood what the problem is. He just kept saying, 'I do things my way. Thank you very much.' Then he'd smile and bow."

Liz floated the scoop of chocolate ice cream around the circumference of the glass and sipped some soda through the straw. Cultural differences? She suddenly thought of Ben. Did she and Ben have cultural differences?

"What did Mr. Lee say?" Liz asked. "Did he take Mr. Kwon's side? I mean, since they're both Asian?"

"Your friend's father?" he asked.

She smiled at her father as if everything was great between her and Ben and said, "Yes, Ben's father."

"Well, Mr. Lee was quiet at the meeting, but he's a quiet man anyway. Actually I'm going over to his restaurant after work. I thought he might have some insight on how we can deal with Mr. Kwon before things get out of hand."

"Out of hand?" Liz asked. "What do you mean?"

"People can be pretty nasty when they're afraid," her father said in a worried voice.

Liz's heart raced. Her father didn't usually talk like that. "What would they do?" she asked.

"I'm not sure. I feel we're on a path toward trouble and that we better change directions now." He reached over and patted his daughter's hand. "But don't you worry. All

you have to be concerned about is school. Tell me, how's it going? Everything okay?"

"Everything's fine, Dad."

She looked into her soda glass, put the straw in her mouth, and took a long sip to wash down the lump in her throat.

THIRTEEN

"Look at this day!" Max Thomas was standing at the opened windows of the art room when Liz and Dary came in. "Come here. All of you."

Dary looked to Liz to see what to do. "Let's go see," she told Dary. They joined Max and the other ten students at the big windows to see what Max saw: the school parking lot bordered on the north by three successive strips of farm fields, each a different shade of brown-green. Beyond the fields the Green Mountains rose—one dark green ridge, then, farther still, a snow-capped blue-green one.

"Splendid," Max said. "Today we begin a unit on landscape. No more models. No more pots of flowers and piles of fruit." His voice rose with enthusiasm, authority, and drama. "We will do landscapes—plein air."

"What's that mean?" Tom asked.

"Plein air, my young friend, is a French phrase for open-air painting. Out in the air. Like the Impressionists. We'll study light." Liz smiled. Max's enthusiasm was catching.

"Elizabeth," Max asked, turning to her, "is this a double period?"

"Yes. It's Thursday."

"Bravo! Get your supplies. Hurry. Hurry. What are you all doing just standing here gazing out the window? Let's get going."

Ten minutes later the twelve students had each chosen a spot behind the school and had set up their pads, charcoal pencils, and boxes of pastels. Dary and Liz were side by side on the stone wall that marked the entrance to the parking lot.

Max fairly danced from student to student, murmuring encouragement: "Draw it as you see it." "Watch what the light does to color." "Is the sky only blue?" "Is the snow only white?"

When he came over to Liz and Dary he said, "Put your heart in your picture, girls, draw what you see with your heart, not just your head and your eyes."

When he left, Dary asked Liz, "Head? Eyes? Heart? Paint body?"

"No," Liz said, laughing, "just what you see." She indicated the panorama before them with a sweep of her arm. "No words today."

Liz continued to sketch the more distant mountain, then the closer one. She kept an eye on how much space she had left for the rest of the scene. She'd decided to ignore the parking lot and make the first farm field the lower edge of her drawing.

After a few minutes she looked over to see what Dary was doing. She hadn't blocked in the mountains. Dary was drawing Brad's green pickup truck. Liz hadn't even noticed it when she looked at the scene before them. But Dary saw it and had filled the whole center portion of her page with its bulky shape.

Liz was about to correct her, to try to explain again what Max meant by a landscape drawing, when she saw that

134

Dary had added a head to her picture—a head without its body—on the ground near the front wheel of the truck. Then the severed torso of the body, chest open with a heart exposed, near the back wheel.

Dary looked up at Brad's truck again. What is she seeing? Liz wondered. Dary drew five men standing in the back of the pickup. They were drawn quickly and in a primitive, childlike style.

Liz swallowed nervously. Dary was slightly turned from her. Liz noticed how rigid Dary's body was. She was obviously seeing something in the parking lot that no one else saw. What should I do? Liz wondered. She thought of getting Max. But he was at the far end of the parking lot working with two other students and she didn't want to leave Dary.

She's drawing from her memory, Liz realized. Her memory of what must have happened in Cambodia.

Liz looked from Dary back to the drawing. One of the figures now held a baby upside down, dangling over the edge of the truck. In the other hand he held a sword, which was halfway through the baby's neck.

Dary was adding more dead bodies and body parts when Max yelled out a new direction to his art students. "If you haven't gotten to color," he instructed cheerfully, "get to it now. Use those pastels and watch the light." Dary didn't even hear.

Liz glanced at her own drawing, barely begun. She opened the box of pastels she shared with Dary and pushed them next to her. "Color," Liz whispered.

Dary looked down at the box and picked out the green. She smeared color all over her drawing of the truck. Then she picked up the red pastel stick. Soon red blood was spurting out of the decapitated head, dropping down the baby's body, lying in puddles on the ground.

When Liz saw that Max was coming toward them she got up to meet him partway. "Isn't this the most amazing day?" he asked her.

"Yes," Liz said. "It is." She put her hand on his arm to stop him from approaching Dary.

He felt and then saw how disturbed Liz was. "What's wrong?" he asked.

"Dary took you literally," Liz told him. "She's drawn from her heart. And it's awful."

"What do you mean?"

"I think she's drawn what happened to her when she was little. She's like in a trance."

Max watched Dary from where they stood. He saw the violent streaks of red on her paper.

"I don't know what to do," Liz said. "I don't know what to say."

"Why don't we see what she says?" Max suggested. "When she finishes. I'm not going to interfere right now. She trusts you more than me."

Liz went back to Dary, who'd finished the drawing and was staring at it.

"Dary," Liz whispered, "what words?"

Dary pointed to the the dangling baby. "Brother," she said. Her finger trailed down to the torso at the wheel of the truck. The word came out in a low groan. "Mother." Then she pointed to the body parts lying around. "All family dead."

"Where's Dary?" Liz asked.

Dary moved her finger to the edge of the page where she'd drawn a row of trees. "Run. Run. Run."

She closed her sketchbook with a gentle thud and turned to Liz. The feeling aroused by her horrid memories showed in her eyes. All the color was draining from her face. "No more words," she whispered. "No more picture."

"Okay, class," Max announced. "Ten-minute call. It's time to pack up and go in."

"Let's go in now," Liz told Dary. "The period's almost over."

Liz wanted to put her arms around Dary, to have her cry in her arms, to comfort her. Instead they walked back into the building in silence—like a funeral procession, Liz thought.

They were putting their art supplies away when Max and the other students came back to the art room. "Are we going to look at what everyone else did?" David was asking Max. "We were all so far away from one another. I don't even know what Liz or Dary were doing."

Someone called out, "Yeah. Let's put them around and look at them."

"No show picture," Dary told Liz in a panicky whisper.

"Next time we'll look at your landscapes," Max told his class. "We'll go back to the parking lot during double period on Monday. You can continue with the picture you're working on or start a new one. Then it'll be your choice what to show the class."

Liz watched Dary reach up and push her closed sketchbook into the painting racks where it would be hidden until Monday among drawings of flowers and vases, fruits and vegetables. Liz knew Dary would never show it to the others. But what would she do with it?

Liz could see how exhausted Dary was from the experience of her drawing. "I'll go with you to your locker," she suggested as they left the room with the other students.

Heading down the corridor to Dary's locker, Liz asked, "Dary, are you okay?"

Dary said, "I okay. Pol Pot no more. Now America. New life."

"Yes," Liz said as she took Dary's hand in hers. "And you have a new friend."

137

Dary gave Liz's hand a squeeze before letting go. "New friend," she repeated. They walked toward Liz's locker.

Ben was sitting on the floor waiting for Liz. I don't believe it, he thought, when he saw the two girls turn the corner into the long corridor. She's with Dary again. He stood up. "I wanted to talk to you," he told Liz when they reached him. "But I guess you're busy."

"I want to talk to you too."

"I go now," Dary said. "Bye."

I can't let her go home alone after what she's just been through, Liz thought. "No," she told Dary. "Wait."

"Can we talk later?" she asked Ben. "Can we meet someplace? Tonight maybe."

Ben thought of how hard it would be to get out of the house on a school night. All the questions that his mother would ask that he would have to answer with lies. "How about the library?" he suggested. "At six-thirty."

Liz thought, he's going to tell his parents he has to do research at the library. He can't admit he's meeting his used-to-be girlfriend who's not Chinese.

"Sewards would be better," Liz challenged. "I have to do something for my father. Besides it's more like halfway between your place and mine. The library is on the other side of town."

"All right. What time?"

"Eight," Liz answered, knowing that would mean Ben would be out long after the eighty-thirty closing of the library, which would make it harder for him to make up a homework-related excuse for not being home. Why am I being so mean to him? she wondered.

I'm going to face up to my mother, Ben thought. "So," he told Liz, "eight o'clock it is."

He ran down the hall so he wouldn't miss the school bus. Why do I feel so angry at Liz? he wondered. It used to feel like love.

"More words?" Dary asked Liz as they started down the hill toward town. "Study more."

"Right," Liz said.

"Brad truck," Dary said.

"What about it?" Liz asked.

"Not bad. Pol Pot truck bad."

"That's right," Liz said.

"Brad not bad," Dary declared.

"That's right," Liz agreed. "Brad is okay."

I may not like the way Brad acts sometimes, Liz thought, but he's certainly not bad.

"Brad okay friend?" Dary asked.

"Yes," Liz answered. "You have many new friends at school."

"You bet," Dary said. "Joey, Terry, David, Spence, Ben . . ."

Liz listened to the litany of at least twenty-five "new friends" Dary claimed after her first two months in Ethan Allen High, Rutland, Vermont, USA. How will she feel, Liz wondered, if on Friday they tell her she has to go to junior high and start over meeting a whole new group of kids?

FOURTEEN

When Liz reached home she noticed her mother's car in the driveway. The house was quiet and her parents' bedroom door was closed. She's taking a nap, Liz concluded as she tiptoed down the hall.

Liz went into her own room, quietly closed the door, then dropped her bookbag on the floor and herself across the bed. What are Ben and I going to talk about tonight? she wondered. I don't even know how I feel about Ben Lee.

She got up, went into the bathroom, and turned on the shower. Maybe, she thought as she took off her clothes, maybe it would be better between Ben and me if Dary and the Korean kids hadn't come to school. She realized that there was a way to send them to a different school. That if she agreed with Ms. Stranton, the principal would arrange for the new Asians to go to the junior high.

I can still be Dary's friend, Liz thought. Dary's been through so much already that changing schools won't be a big deal. Besides it'll probably be better for her to get extra

help in English from Ms. Stranton than from me. And maybe my own schoolwork is suffering.

Liz pictured elegant, mature Dary in a seventh grade gym class. Or in line in the junior high cafeteria. She let the water run over her head and face, trying to wash away the caption for those images that would ask, *What's wrong with this picture?*

Brad was straightening out the light bulb display at Hadley's Hardware. After an hour of reorganizing the gallon paint cans in the supply room, working with the featherweight boxes of light bulbs was like not working at all.

Things are getting better for me, Brad thought. Mr. Madison liked that I did my English homework even though I was suspended. Liz had lunch with me today. I got new friends with these Korean kids. Helping Jae-Hyuk and Soon-Je with English will help me do better in school and with Liz. My only problem is that chink. Before bending down to get another stack of light bulbs out of the carton, Brad tried a karate move that Jae-Hyuk taught him. I can learn karate, he thought. Jae-Hyuk's a great guy. I have a lot to teach him and he has a lot to teach me.

Mr. Hadley came down the aisle with a box of fluorescent lights he wanted Brad to add to the display. "What're you whistling about?" he asked Brad.

"Nothing special."

"Don't let me stop you," Mr. Hadley said. "I just wonder what anyone has to be happy about in this town."

Brad looked at him. "What's wrong with this town?"

"Those Koreans," Mr. Hadley said with an edge. "They're making all sorts of trouble."

"What trouble?" Brad asked. "What'd they do?"

"Just ruining business for everyone in downtown, that's all."

142

"Ruining business? But there was a fruit and vegetable store there before. What's the difference?"

Mr. Hadley *harrumphed* as he picked up a light bulb and showed it to Brad. "I'll bet you pretty soon they'll be selling bulbs and beer and cigarettes and stuff that'll compete with the rest of us. I see nothing but trouble ahead."

"What kind of trouble do you mean?"

"They're going to be open twenty-four hours a day. Damn fool idea. Now what kind of people do you think that'll bring to town? Things were fine just the way they were before they came. Don't know why folks like that can't just stay put in their own country. Asians are taking over America. It's an Asian invasion." He was practically yelling.

"Mr. Hadley"—Brad tried to keep his own voice level—"I don't know what you're getting so upset about. The Kwons are nice people. I'm friends with their kids. It seems to me that they've got as much right to run a business in Rutland as anyone else."

Mr. Hadley's body tensed as his voice rose angrily. "Listen, I'm telling you I don't like those people being here."

"Well I think that's a prejudiced way to talk. If you talk like that you'll just stir up trouble yourself. They're not making any trouble."

"They're making trouble for you, mister," Mr. Hadley said, poking his big index finger in Brad's chest. "Because if I hear any more stupid talk like that from you, you can go get your paycheck from your little yellow friends."

The front bell *binged*, signaling an entering customer.

"Why are you talking about them like that?" Brad asked. "All they did was buy a store. What's the crime?"

"You don't understand," Mr. Hadley said as he moved off to meet his customer. "But you will. They're taking over and your generation is the one that's going to suffer."

Brad watched Mr. Hadley's back. I could lose my job over this, he thought. "Little yellow friends," what a sick thing to say.

Then, like a 150-watt bulb lighting up in his head, Brad heard Mr. Hadley's words echo in his own. Ben Lee. He was yellow too. But he was no friend. He always made him feel stupid and he was competition for Liz. That guy's been bugging me, Brad concluded, wherever he comes from.

A thin cloud of steam from clear chicken broth enveloped Ben as he went through the living room toward the kitchen. His mother was straining the broth at the stove. "Mmm," he told her, "smells good."

"Special chicken dish for you tonight," she said with a warm smile. "Sit. You can have a cup of broth before you study."

"Thanks." Ben sat on the edge of the kitchen chair and nervously ran his hand through his hair.

"How are you, Mom?" he asked in Chinese.

"You speak Chinese?" his mother answered with a scowl. "Must want something from me."

"I know you like me not to forget my Chinese heritage," Ben answered in fractured Mandarin.

"Too late," his mother said. She placed a bowl of steaming broth in front of him. "Besides why we here? We here for you to be an American. The smartest American in the whole of United States."

"I don't get it," Ben said in English. "A week ago you were complaining that I was too American."

"I think about it after. You have Chinese in you. You have Chinese on you. Nobody ever not know this is a Chinese boy. If you want to think you're Mr. Robert Redford or Mr. Paul Newman, you can think so. But always I know and everybody else knows—you are Chinese. Maybe

144

you stupid-acting Chinese. Maybe you rude-to-mother Chinese. But you Chinese."

Ben gulped the last of his broth. He controlled the frustration and anger he felt. "I have to do my homework now," he said. "So I'm going to my room." What am I so afraid of? he wondered as he stood up. My friends talk straight to their mothers. I can do it too. He told his mother, "After dinner tonight I've got to go out."

"Got to?" she asked. "How come? What's so important to go out on homework night?"

"I had a fight with someone. I want to straighten it out."

Alarmed, Tia put up her fists and shadowboxed the air over the table. "Fight like this?"

"No. No. With words."

"With words is called argument, no?"

"You're right. It was an argument," Ben said.

"See, I know English better than you. Chinese mothers are very smart."

I know you're smart, Ben thought. Too smart to outsmart. "So I'm going out to settle this argument. I won't be late."

"Tell me about argument, then we'll see how important you should go."

"No," Ben said. "It's not about the family. It's not so important to you. It's important to me and it's private."

"You have secret?"

"Yes," he said. "I do."

"Another bigshot American idea," she said, "to have secret from family." She looked sad.

Ben felt sad himself as he left the kitchen. At first he thought it was because of his argument with Liz, but by the time he sat down at his desk to do his homework he realized he was sad because he had a secret from his mother.

145

When Dary came into the apartment and heard her aunt and uncle in the kitchen speaking in Khmer her brain relaxed. Oh how I love to hear my language, she thought. To understand all the words and to know the words for all my thoughts. She joined them at the kitchen table, anxious to get in on the Khmer talk before her aunt and uncle went to work and she'd be alone with her cousins, who liked to speak only English.

For a few minutes she sipped tea and listened. Uncle told Aunt about the patients he took care of as a nurse's aide at Rutland Nursing Home. How he always knew what the doctors would say about a patient's treatment before they said it. Aunt said Uncle should study to be a doctor like he planned to be in Cambodia. But Uncle protested he was lucky to have a job at all. Someday, Aunt said, when you learn English very well, maybe you can go to medical school in this country. Uncle said that it would be too expensive, that they must work hard so their children would have a good education, an opportunity neither of them had.

"You are right," Aunt agreed. "We are here by a miracle. A miracle so that our children can have a chance." Uncle got up and told Dary and his wife, "I have to go to work now." And he left to do a night shift at the home.

Aunt poured Dary more tea. "You are our daughter. You will have all the advantages that our sons have. There will be no difference in how we treat you. Maybe you'll be a doctor. My sister's spirit would be so happy to see such a successful daughter."

"Aunt," Dary asked in a respectful voice, "how did I run away when my mother was killed by the Khmer Rouge?"

Aunt leaned forward and looked into her niece's eyes. She knew Dary had finally remembered consciously what they'd seen together.

"Today I remember," Dary said. "For the first time. I see the whole thing in a picture. I remembered it in English words, not Khmer words. There is a green truck. I see the body of my mother. The body of my baby brother. And many, many more. I was a baby then so I now wonder, how did I run?" Dary added in English, "Mother dead. Why not me dead?"

Her aunt told Dary the story in a whisper, keeping her voice low and soft so that the retelling would not disturb the spirits of grandparents, parents, brothers, sister, husband, children, and so many aunts and uncles.

"At that time," she began, "there was much gossip coming to our village about the Khmer Rouge and Pol Pot. All bad. We think we must run, but we did not know where to go because in all the villages it was the same. Everywhere the Khmer Rouge were coming. But when Khmer Rouge got closer to our village we thought our only hope is to hide in a cave.

"That day I took you and went to look for a cave in the mountain area near our village. Everyone else stayed in the village to get ready to leave. Your mother was going to cook and pack for leaving and she had your baby brother to feed at the breast. I took you with me so she could work faster and also because you were so cute and good company. We looked all day for a cave. But no place was big enough to hide in. So I went back to our village with you to tell the family that I didn't find a hiding place. You are tied to my back by then because you were so tired from walking. You were so heavy that I thought, maybe I was foolish to take her with me. Maybe if I was alone I could have looked more and found a big cave. I know now that it was to save you that I got that idea to take you with me."

Dary thought, because if I'd stayed with my mother I'd be dead.

147

"We came through woods," her aunt continued. "I heard strange noises like I'd never heard before. Shouting, angry, angry. And moans, like sorrow no one should know in this life. I saw. I saw it all. I wanted to cover your eyes, but I'm afraid you'll cry. I think, she's just a baby so maybe she doesn't understand. I turned from the place quickly. I ran. You saved my life."

"How could I save your life?" Dary asked. "I was heavy, making it hard for you to run."

"Because I only ran to save you. Otherwise I would go to die with my family—my husband, my sister, my mother, my father."

Aunt looked down at her hands and sighed. A sigh to remember all the loved people she'd lost.

"Then what happened?" Dary asked. "I wasn't with you for so many years."

"For a long time we ran. Then we were caught. I thought they would kill us. But no, they sent me to Khmer Rouge camp for women. They sent you to camp for children. Many, many died in the camps. But I am strong and work hard. By luck I lived and escaped that camp and went to a border camp in Thailand. Luck stayed with me—I meet a new husband and have two babies in that camp and now I am here.

She leaned closer to her niece. "Your luck is good too. I thought for many years that you must be dead. Then I saw your picture in the Red Cross article. I knew your face no matter how much you'd grown. The church helped me bring you here. Dary, much luck comes to you and me. Luck from your mother's spirit. She's with us all the time."

Dary looked around at the kitchen. She saw the food and pans her aunt had laid out ready for cooking dinner. She heard the noisy entrance of her cousins Phroh and Arn coming in from school, happy to be home. She felt the love

of her aunt who knew her when she was a baby. She remembered the touch of Liz's hand when she called her friend. And she felt, deep inside, the spirit of her mother.

"Yes, I have good luck too," she told her aunt.

Aunt stood up and straightened out her pink nylon Sewards uniform. "I have to go to work."

Phroh came running into the kitchen. "What's going on? What's for supper?" Seeing that his mother was ready for work he added, "Is Dary cooking?"

"You bet," Dary answered in English.

"Great," Phroh said as he ran back into the living room. "We're watching TV. Call us when it's ready."

Dary went to the doorway between the kitchen and living room. Phroh and Arn were already stretched out on the floor facing the television. Above the noise of the cartoons Dary called out in English, "No way. No TV. Homework. After supper you do dish. I do homework."

"No fair," Arn said. "You're older."

"And you're the girl," Phroh added.

"This America," Dary said. "Boy clean dish like girl."

The two boys complained loudly in Khmer to their mother.

Aunt smiled at Dary, then spoke sternly to her sons in English. "Dary's the boss of you two. She shows you how to clean dish. I think good idea."

The boys moaned. Aunt turned off the TV on her way out. Dary went back to the kitchen humming the theme song from the television show the boys had been watching.

Liz was making herself a peanut butter and jelly sandwich when her mother came into the kitchen. "I fell asleep," her mother said matter-of-factly as she turned on the gas burner under the teapot.

"You had today off?" Liz asked.

"Yes. I love afternoon naps." She looked her daughter

149

over. "How are you doing? You going over to the store to finish the window?"

Liz nodded. "Then I'm meeting Ben at Sewards. Okay?"

"Don't you have homework?"

"I did it already."

Her mother sat down to wait for the water to boil. Liz was about to tell her mother about Dary and the picture she'd drawn, but before she could begin her mother asked, "Don't we have a rule that you don't have dates on school nights?"

Liz looked at her mother and nodded.

"So maybe tonight you and Ben can talk on the phone and wait until the weekend for your date."

I understand why Ben lies to his parents, Liz thought. If I'd just said I was going to the library I wouldn't be having this stupid conversation.

"Mom, it's not really a date. I'm going to be downtown anyway. Sewards is close by. I'll be home by ten. It's not like we're going to the movies or something."

"It's setting a precedent," her mother insisted.

"It isn't. I promise."

"Just remember, Elizabeth, you have brains and we want you to go to college and have a career in science. There's a lot of competition, especially with these new Asian students. Mark my words, they'll learn English—thanks to you—and be right up there competing with you for the math and science prizes. You could use scholarship money too. At this stage of your life you should be using your energies on yourself, not others."

Liz was so annoyed by her mother's speech that a lump of peanut butter sandwich stuck in her throat. She swallowed it down with a gulp of milk before saying, "Mom, I'm Dary's only real friend. She's had this horrible life. She deserves to be able to learn English and compete."

"You can be her friend without spending all your free time helping her learn English. There are people who are trained and paid to do that."

Tears leaked over the edges of Liz's eyelids and trickled down her face. "You don't really believe in my intelligence if you don't think I can balance out doing my own work and helping Dary. I can't believe you don't trust me enough to figure something like that out for myself."

Her mother went over to her and put her arm around her shoulder. "Sweetie, of course I trust you. I just want what's best for you. I'm on your side, remember?"

"I think . . ." Liz said, "I think that if you're on my side you should trust me to do what's right in my schoolwork and let me decide where I want to go to college and what kind of a career I want to have. And certainly you can trust me to figure out for myself how much to help Dary." She shook off her mother's arm and went upstairs to wash the tears off her face.

As Diane sat down to drink her tea she felt saddened that her daughter had gotten so angry. I'm only trying to help, she thought. Why is she so upset?

Half an hour later Liz sat cross-legged in the store window between the fashionably shod paws of Mrs. Rabbit and Mr. Rabbit. I'm so grumpy and tense, Liz thought, maybe working with the letters and thinking about how to place them on the window will help me relax.

She was looking down at the letters on the floor when Brad drove his pickup truck into the parking space in front of Kwon's market. Brad didn't see Liz either. He was hurrying to warn the Kwons about how Mr. Hadley was out to get them.

When he stepped out of the truck Brad noticed the lights on in the shoe store window spotlighting Mr. and Mrs.

Rabbit. He squinted. Was he seeing things? Was that a doll that looked just like Liz sitting on the floor of the display? He looked again. It moved. It was Liz. He ran across the street and rapped on the window.

Liz looked up. Brad was grinning at her through the glass. "I thought you were a statue," he shouted, pointing to the stuffed animals. "Like in the book with the rabbit."

"*Alice in Wonderland?*" Liz guessed.

He nodded, smiling. She noticed the pickup parked across the street and remembered Dary's drawing. I've got to tell him, she thought, it's only fair. She motioned for Brad to come into the store.

He poked his head into the display. "Hi," he said. "What're you doing?"

She pointed to the letters. "Putting up a saying about spring."

"Thanks for giving me all those homework questions," he said. "I think I'll pass the course."

"That's great, Brad," she told him. She thought about how awful it must feel to sit through classes when you're failing.

"I'm studying a lot harder than I used to," he told her.

"Are you here to help Soon and Jae with their English?" She didn't add, *You'd be better off spending more time doing your own schoolwork.* Liz realized that she almost sounded just like her mother.

"I have to talk to them about something. But then I saw you and came over to say hi."

Liz looked at her watch. She'd never get the window finished if she didn't start and she still wanted to explain to Brad about Dary. "Could you sit there?" she asked, pointing to a corner of the display, "and hand me those pieces of tape? It'll only take a minute."

"Sure." He crawled over the shoes in the display and sat down cross-legged in the corner.

Liz's father looked into the display. "Hi, Brad."

"Hi, Mr. Gaynor."

"How are things at the hardware store?" Tom asked, hoping for a clue to just how crazy Hadley was getting over the Korean market issue.

"Not very good," Brad answered.

"How's that?"

"Mr. Hadley's being real mean and prejudiced about the Koreans coming here. He's telling all his customers not to shop there. It's disgusting."

Liz was surprised to hear Brad's comments. Is this the same Brad who accused Ben of giving him a flat tire and called him slant-eyes and chink?

"Well, Hadley's certainly getting this thing all out of proportion," her father said. "The Chamber of Commerce is meeting later to see what we can do to calm things down." He went back to the counter to finish closing up the register for the day.

Brad handed Liz another piece of tape. "I think that Soon-Je should go to the meeting with her father," he said. "She'll understand the English better than her father does. I could help too."

"Good idea," Liz agreed.

"After all they're my friends," Brad concluded. "I can't let anybody push them around."

Maybe I've underestimated Brad, Liz thought as she stuck another letter on the glass. "Listen, I know why Dary gets so upset when she sees you. It doesn't have to do with you, Brad. Not at all."

Liz explained how Dary's association with a green pickup truck was connected to her devastating experience during the war in Cambodia. Until today Dary didn't even know

why the truck had upset her. Brad listened attentively as Liz explained what had happened with Dary.

Meanwhile, Ben was walking down Main Street on his way to Sewards. He was determined to make things right with Liz, to talk out their misunderstandings and problems. He'd dealt with his mother. Now he'd be able to face Liz. He glanced at the shoe store display as he passed. Liz did such a great job. And there she was standing in the middle of it. His heart skipped a beat. I know I care for her. Maybe I even love her, he thought as he started across the street to the shoe store. I've even gone against my parents for her, he repeated to himself. Suddenly he noticed that Brad was sitting at Liz's feet, looking up intently at her. Both of their faces were filled with emotion. Ben felt his heart sink and felt sick to his stomach. He couldn't believe it. Why has she been bothering with me, he wondered, when it's so clear that she likes him? Am I her pet Chinaman? A china doll for her collection, like Dary? He went back across the street, gave Brad's tire a good kick, and headed home.

"Do you think I should paint my truck another color?" Brad was asking Liz. "So it won't remind her so much of what happened?"

"No. I think now that Dary's remembered and knows why your truck upset her that it won't bother her as much. Maybe not at all."

As Liz stuck the letter S on the window she looked across the street at Brad's truck. She saw Ben. He was breaking into a fast walk, almost a run, and she realized that he'd just seen her with Brad.

"I gotta go," she told Brad.

"What about the window?"

She'd already stepped over him and down out of the display.

"I'm late," she explained. "Thanks for helping. Tell

my father I'll finish the window later." She raced out the door.

She ran a block, calling, "Ben, Ben, wait." Ben didn't turn around until she caught up with him at the traffic light.

"Where are you going?" she asked.

"Home," he answered. "Look, I know what's going on."

"You and I had a date, or an appointment, whatever it was. Why are you going home?"

"You and Brad. I saw you together."

"So what if I was talking to Brad? I told you a hundred times he's a friend. He might have a thing for me, but I'm totally not interested in him as a boyfriend." She hated how edgy and angry her voice sounded.

"Well I don't know why you bother with someone like him," he said.

"Just because you think he's stupid doesn't mean I'm not going to talk to him. The person I don't feel like talking to tonight is you. I mean I do but I don't. I hate it when you're so high and mighty, like you're better than everyone else." She started to cross the street in angry strides.

Ben grabbed her arm. "Wait. You can't just walk away like that," he yelled.

"You were walking away from me," she yelled back.

"What's happening here, Liz?" he lowered his voice and tried to get her to look at him, but she turned away. "I don't get it. We were great friends when we were just science partners."

"Maybe we should go back to being just science partners then," she answered.

"Maybe I've been acting like a jerk," he said. "I promised myself we'd have a calm talk, get everything out in the open, and now I'm acting like a jealous boyfriend. Let's go

155

someplace where we can talk. Aren't we friends enough to do that?"

They walked together back through Main Street toward the small town green in the center of town. There was an awkward silence between them, neither of them knowing where to begin. Neither of them wanting to start by talking about Brad. Liz finally said, "Dary."

"What about her?"

"The day she came you started acting funny. Funny-weird. Why did you mind her so much?"

"Because everyone put us together. Even Mr. Madison."

They'd reached the green and sat side by side on a park bench.

"I guess I did that too," Liz confessed. "I was threatened by the idea . . . the idea of you and Dary. When I first saw her sitting in my seat, next to you, I figured she'd be more your friend than I was, that you'd like her better than me because she was Asian."

"That's what everyone does. That's what I was telling you the other day. They're grouping me with other Asians. Assuming we'll be together—like a clique. Before Dary came I was just one of the guys. Now I'm being treated like another Asian right off the boat. A new immigrant. No separate identity. No Americanness. I hate it."

"So that's why you avoid me when I'm with Dary?" Liz asked.

"I guess so. Why'd you volunteer to take care of her like that anyway?" Ben asked.

"I needed the service credit."

"That's all?"

"Well, now I do it because I like Dary. It's fascinating to watch her learning English. When I saw that you disapproved of my being with her I wasn't going to stop helping

her just to please you. I hate it when women do things like that. I mean, how could you respect me if I was such a wimp?"

Ben grinned.

"What? What's funny?"

"I like you. You're right. I wouldn't respect you if you did things like that." Ben pointed toward the white marble town hall at the head of the green. A group of five people was climbing the steps to the front entrance. "Isn't that your father?" Ben asked. He tensed. "And Brad and the Kwons?" He turned to Liz. "What's going on?"

"They're going to a Chamber of Commerce meeting. There's a problem with the Kwons. Brad's boss, Mr. Hadley, wants to ruin business for the Kwons and make trouble."

"Brad is going to the meeting too?"

"He wants to be sure that the Kwons understand what's going on. It was his idea that Soon-Je could help her father with the language problem. He's disgusted with Mr. Hadley and how prejudiced he is. Honest. He's being nice."

"Maybe someone should remind Brad how prejudiced he is himself," Ben told her.

"I think you're being unfair to Brad. You complain about his insults to you, but you insult him all the time. I'm not saying I don't do it too. But you don't let up. You're always saying he's stupid by calling him things like 'pea-brained.' That's stereotyping too."

"Are you forgetting all the racist slurs he's said to me?" Ben asked.

"No I'm not. But between you and Brad I don't even remember who started it. Was it him insulting you or you insulting him? All I know is I hate being caught in the crossfire."

"But Brad's so stupid he—" Ben stopped himself midsentence. "I see what you mean," he said softly.

Liz noticed Mr. Lee crossing the green. "There's your father."

"I guess he's going to the meeting too." Ben could see that his father would be walking right past them, which meant he'd see them sitting on the bench together.

"Should we tell him we're studying?" Liz asked Ben conspiratorially. "I don't even have a pencil with me."

"No problem," Ben said but he was nervously rubbing his hand on his thighs as his father approached.

Liz wondered what excuse Ben would use to cover up for being alone in the park with a girl—a Caucasian girl—on a school night.

"Hi, Dad," Ben said.

Mr. Lee stopped in front of them.

"This is my friend Elizabeth Gaynor," Ben said.

Liz stood up and shook hands with Mr. Lee.

"Nice to meet you, Elizabeth," he said. "I know your father. You and Ben are science partners, I hear."

"That's right," Liz said. "We're studying—"

Ben interrupted, "But we're not studying now. We're on a date."

Mr. Lee muttered something in Chinese to Ben. Then to Liz he said, "Nice to meet you. I'm on my way to a meeting with your father and other businessmen now." He smiled good-bye and continued across the green.

"What'd he say to you in Chinese?" Liz asked Ben.

"He asked me if I'd done my homework."

Liz laughed. "That's what my mother asked me when I said I was meeting you."

Ben put his hand on hers. They looked into each other's eyes. "Maybe," Liz said, "Chinese Americans and Italian/ Irish Americans aren't so different."

"Different enough to make it interesting," Ben commented.

"Maybe we should go someplace else. How about going to Sewards like we planned?"

"You know what I'd like to do?" Liz said. "I'd like to go to that meeting and see what happens."

Ben nodded in agreement even though he would have preferred just spending some time alone with Liz. "My father will think it's a pretty strange date!" he said with a laugh. They held hands as they walked along the gravel path that cut through the green. Going up the steps toward the town hall entrance Ben turned to Liz. "This weekend let's go on a real date, okay?"

"Okay," Liz agreed and smiled.

Tom Gaynor, as current president of the Chamber of Commerce, sat at a table facing the twenty-one members in attendance. Brad sat in the third row with Mr. Kwon and Soon-Je. Mr. Hadley, who sat across the aisle from them, kept giving Brad threatening sidelong glances. Brad leaned over and told Soon-Je, "It's important to explain everything."

Soon-Je spoke in Korean to her father. He answered his daughter while flashing a friendly smile at Brad.

"What'd he say?" Brad asked.

"I tell him that you go against boss to help us," she said. "He say you are a life friend of Kwon family."

Brad's face flushed. He felt good, brave and determined. No matter how long it takes, he thought, or what Mr. Hadley says or if I never can get a job again, I'm going to make sure that the Kwons are treated fairly.

As Tom Gaynor lowered the gavel to signal the beginning of the meeting he looked up to see his daughter and Ben Lee standing in the doorway. He motioned for them to come in and sit in the back.

Mr. Hadley saw them too. "I'd like to raise an objection before we begin," he called out without asking to be recognized. "I move that this be a closed meeting." He glared at

Brad. "And that nonmembers—including the Korean kid—be told to leave."

There was some discussion but the final vote was six in favor of closing the meeting to nonmembers, fifteen in favor of keeping it opened to the public. As Ben and Liz took seats in the back, Ben's father turned around and nodded at them.

Brad was glad Liz was there. But he wondered if Ben would cause him problems as usual. The important thing, Brad decided, was to sit tight and help the Kwons the best he could.

The meeting began with several merchants presenting their objections to the Kwons' store, including their concern about how the long business hours would affect their own businesses and the reputation of downtown.

Each time a point was made Brad told Soon-Je, "Translate it into Korean for your father. Be sure he understands." When Soon-Je didn't understand, Brad explained to her in simpler English than the speaker used, and then she would translate for her father. If her father had a response he spoke in his own English. If there were any questions about what Mr. Kwon meant Soon-Je or Brad would elaborate for the members.

At one point Mr. Hadley stood and shouted, "Doesn't anybody here understand? They're going to take over. We'll have a regular little Chinatown right here in Rutland. Don't you realize that?"

Brad stood up too. "The Kwons aren't Chinese, Mr. Hadley," he said. "They're Korean. And what if they were Chinese? The Lees are Chinese. They've been in business in this town for two years. There've been no problems."

"You," Hadley yelled. "You disloyal SOB You have no business speaking at this meeting."

Loud shouts from other members of the Chamber of Commerce were interrupted by the sharp bang of a gavel.

Mr. Lee put up his hand. Ben watched anxiously as his father rose to speak.

"The chair recognizes Mr. Lee," Tom Gaynor said with another bang of the gavel.

Except for an occasional mumble from Mr. Hadley the room became quiet.

"The young man is correct," Mr. Lee began. "Chinese is not Korean. Any more than Irish is Italian or French is Russian. In Asia sometimes Koreans and Chinese don't get along. I am not Korean. I am Chinese. I am American. But I say a person should have the right to prove themself. Where a person comes from makes no difference. What's your nationality makes no difference. Only difference is what you do when you come here. And what you do to make good opportunity in life for your children." He nodded and sat down.

Liz leaned over and whispered to Ben, "That was great." He nodded. She saw Ben smile proudly.

Fifteen minutes later the secret votes had been counted. Tom Gaynor looked around at the gathering, cleared his throat and began. "The vote is seventeen to four in favor of the proposition that the Chamber of Commerce officially welcome the Kwon business to Main Street and that the Chamber assist them in any way we can. As president of the local chapter of the Chamber of Commerce I welcome the Kwon family business to Main Street and offer them a voting membership in the Chamber of Commerce." He nodded at Mr. Kwon, "We thank you for accepting our recommendation that your store be open fifteen hours a day rather than twenty-four hours."

Everyone applauded. Mr. Hadley got up, "Big mistake,"

he mumbled loudly. "Big mistake." With a final scowl at Brad he walked out of the room.

That's it, Brad thought, there goes my job. Right out the door. His heart sank. And there goes my pickup truck too.

After a final thud of the gavel Tom announced, "This meeting is adjourned."

Mr. Lee walked over to Mr. Kwon and shook hands with him. "Happy to have you on Main Street. Maybe we can order some vegetables and other Asian foods together."

Mr. Kwon smiled broadly. "Good. Make business. This my daughter." Soon-Je nodded at Mr. Lee. "And this my friend, Brad Mulville."

Brad shook Mr. Lee's hand. "Hi. I like your restaurant, especially that chow mein stuff."

Mr. Lee smiled. "Next time you are in the restaurant tell me hello and I'll give you something very special, better than chow mein 'stuff.' You were strong to help your friend when your boss, Mr. Hadley, was acting so crazy."

Tom Gaynor joined them and put his arm around Brad's shoulder. "You were terrific, Brad. If Hadley fires you or makes it hard for you at work because of tonight, I'm sure we can find an after-school job for you somewhere on Main Street."

Brad looked around at the smiling faces turned on him and thought, this is great. All these people like me. Then he saw Ben Lee walking toward him.

As Ben approached Brad a series of memories flashed through his mind under a soundtrack of racist slurs. Brad cutting in on him when he was dancing with Liz. Brad accusing him of slashing his tire. Brad holding him by the collar and throwing him on the snowy street. But he also remembered his own comments about Brad's lack of brain power and how he made a fool of him over the flat tire. He remembered his own attitude of superiority.

He went up to Brad who was looking at him quizzically—waiting to see what Ben's first move would be—not wanting to have an argument or fight in front of all his new friends.

Ben extended his hand, "Congratulations, Brad. You were terrific."

Brad shook Ben's hand, still not sure whether an insult would follow or if Ben was putting him on like about the flat tire.

Liz said, "You were great, Brad. The way you stood up to Mr. Hadley was amazing." And, "You were great too, Dad," Liz told Tom Gaynor, "I never saw you run a meeting before."

"So," Brad said looking directly at Liz, "anybody need a ride home while I've still got the truck?"

"Liz can come home with me," her father interjected. "Car's right down the block."

Ben looked at his watch. It was only nine o'clock. "We still have time to go to Sewards," he whispered to Liz.

Liz turned to Brad and her father. "I'm going to Sewards with Ben."

"Sewards?" Soon-Je asked. "What that mean?"

"It's an ice cream store," Liz explained. "We go there to buy ice cream cones and sundaes. It's very good."

"I like ice cream," Soon-Je said.

"I told Mom I'd be home by ten," Liz explained to her father. "She said it was okay."

Soon-Je was smiling around at all of them. How nice, she thought, they invite me to go to Sewards with them. She asked her father something in Korean. He answered her.

"What did you say?" Brad asked her.

"I tell him young people go to Sewards for ice cream and be home at ten. He say okay if I'm with family friend,

163

Brad." She beamed. Brad shrugged his shoulders and looked questioningly at Liz and Ben. Liz nudged Ben.

"I guess we're all going to Sewards," Ben said, wondering if he'd ever be alone with Liz.

When they got to Sewards Liz moved into the booth expecting Ben to sit next to her, but Soon-Je was there first. "I sit by you," she said. Liz looked up at Ben and smiled as he moved into the seat across from her and made room for Brad. Brad gave him a friendly tap on the arm with his fist. "So buddy," Brad asked, "how's it going?"

After they ordered sundaes, Liz excused herself to go to the bathroom. To get to the ladies' room she passed the soda fountain counter. Mrs. Dahm was clearing away dishes and wiping off the counter.

"Hello," Liz greeted her. "How's Dary?"

"Dary busy with Phroh and Arn and homework," she explained. "English better every day, thank you. Nice to be with kids own age."

"Yes," Liz said, "it is." She watched for a moment as Mrs. Dahm worked. "The Pol Pot time was a very hard time for Dary," Liz finally said. "She's a very strong girl."

Mrs. Dahm leaned forward and spoke softly, "Pol Pot time is hard time for every person in Cambodia. To live is miracle. Must be thankful."

"Dary drew a picture," Liz continued, "of a pickup truck and soldiers killing people."

"I know," Mrs. Dahm said. "I am with her then. I am with her now. I tell her, do not worry about past. You her friend. We thank you always."

A cheery man at the other end of the counter called out, "How about some Dahm service down here?"

Mrs. Dahm laughed and answered him, "You bet." She turned back to Liz. "He makes joke about name all the

time. Doesn't mean to insult. Is like on American TV show and movies. People make jokes with waitress." She headed toward her customer.

When Liz got back to the booth Soon-Je was describing to Ben and Brad what it was like to go to school in New York City. Ben started talking about schools in Chicago.

"I've always been here in Vermont," Brad said. "Like Liz." He turned to face Ben. "Guess what? I'm learning karate."

Ben and Liz exchanged surprised kicks under the table.

"I don't want to fight with you, Brad," Ben said evenly.

"I didn't mean karate to fight. I meant to like practice together. Jae-Hyuk's a black belt. Maybe the three of us could even start a school, after I learn karate and Jae-Hyuk learns English. We could open a place on Main Street." He was beaming. "I got lots of friends in the business community."

"I'm pretty busy studying," Ben said.

"Oh," Brad said. "Me too." But he was disappointed. He'd been feeling good to be included as part of the group. Ben must really not like me, he thought. "Maybe I wasn't so nice to you sometimes," he told Ben, "but man, you made me feel like a fool. Like I'm stupid or something. And in front of everyone."

Ben nodded. "I guess we both said and did things we're sorry for."

"I guess," Brad agreed. "Let's start over."

They firmly gripped each other's hand and shook.

Liz looked from one to the other. Ben, so smart and sweet. Brad, maybe not so dumb after all, and sweet too.

Brad smiled broadly at Liz, Ben, and Soon-Je. "Everyone's the same, don't you think? We're all from different countries, but right now we're here together. Sewards Dairy, Main Street, Rutland, Vermont, USA, Planet Earth."

Twenty minutes later they paid the check and left.

They came through the swinging door of Sewards into the crisp, clean air. As Brad looked up at the star-splattered sky he didn't feel so bad. "You know, I've lost my job and my pickup truck, but I'm glad I've got friends," he said. He didn't add how glad he was to have Liz back. Maybe not as a girlfriend, but as a friend. He remembered how when they were little they played in her backyard with his trucks and that Liz was the only one he'd let play with his backhoe. He was glad he always lived in Rutland and not in Chicago or New York or Korea.

"Time to get going," Ben said as he looked at his watch. "I'll walk you home, Liz." He took her hand.

"Good night, Soon-Je," Liz said. "Bye, Brad."

"See you in school tomorrow," Ben added.

Soon-Je looked around at the three smiling faces. "I love it here in America," she said. Brad and Ben and Liz smiled. "I am lucky," she said. "You have been lucky to be born here. I am lucky now."

"We're all lucky in some way," Liz said.

Brad gave Ben a friendly pat on the back and looked from him to Liz. "So, are you two going out together?"

"Yes," Ben said. "We are."

The night air smelled sweet as Liz and Ben walked hand in hand down the street. Liz took a deep breath and squeezed Ben's hand.

"Ben," she said, "tell me it isn't spring."

ABOUT THE AUTHOR

Jeanne Betancourt has written thirteen novels for young adults and younger readers, as well as original teleplays on themes similar to those in her books, including *Teen Father*, *Don't Touch*, *Supermom's Daughter*, and *Tattle*. Her work has been nominated for six Emmys and two Humanitas Awards, and she is the recipient of the National Psychological Association's award for Excellence in the Media.

Jeanne Betancourt's other Bantam Starfire books are *Not Just Party Girls*, *Home Sweet Home*, and *Sweet Sixteen and Never . . .* , a Children's Choice Award winner.

Ms. Betancourt taught English in junior and senior high schools for sixteen years before devoting herself full-time to writing. She lives in New York City and rural Connecticut with her husband, Lee Minoff, and has a daughter in college.

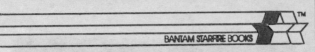

Other Bantam Starfire Books you will enjoy

SWEET SIXTEEN AND NEVER
  by Jeanne Betancourt
HOME SWEET HOME by Jeanne Betancourt
LANDING ON MARVIN GARDENS
  by Rona S. Zable
SAVING LENNY by Margaret Willey
DEFINITELY NOT SEXY by Jane Sutton
US AGAINST THEM by Michael French
SUDDENLY SUPER RICH
  by Gloria D. Miklowitz
PEOPLE LIKE US by Barbara Cohen
THE YEAR OF THE GOPHER
  by Phyllis Reynolds Naylor
FORBIDDEN CITY by William Bell

Her father looked up from the front page of the newspaper he'd been scanning. "You know what I think? I think there's a prejudice towards Ben."

"There is," Liz said. She was about to tell them about the way Brad and some of the other kids called Ben "chink" and "Chinaman." And how, in a way, her mother's behavior was insulting to Ben. But she didn't get a chance because her father kept talking. "I'm glad you recognize that, Elizabeth. It's a subtle prejudice, I'm sure. Maybe the teachers don't even realize they're doing it. The expectation now is that an Asian will do better in math and science than one of our own."

Remembering what Mr. Hadley said to Ben at the hardware store, Liz said, "A lot of people think that but—"

"That's right," her mother interrupted. "And they give him better grades because they expect him to do better than you. That's why so many Asians are walking away with all those science and math awards . . . and, I might add, scholarships. It's very unfair to you. And to American kids. You're the ones who suffer from the prejudice."

"That's crazy," Liz said. "That's not what I meant. It's not *me* they're prejudiced against. It's Ben. Everyone treats him like he's different when he's just another American kid."

"Is he?" her mother asked.

"Yes," Liz answered with a snap. "He is."

MORE THAN MEETS THE EYE

A Bantam Book
Bantam hardcover edition / June 1990
Bantam paperback edition / December 1991

The Starfire logo is a registered trademark of Bantam Books, a division of
Bantam Doubleday Dell Publishing Group, Inc. Registered in U.S. Patent
and Trademark offices and elsewhere.

ISBN 0-553-29351-6

Published simultaneously in the United States and Canada

Bantam Books are published by Bantam Books, a division of Bantam Doubleday
Dell Publishing Group, Inc. Its trademark, consisting of the words "Bantam
Books" and the portrayal of a rooster, is Registered in U.S. Patent and Trademark
Office and in other countries. Marca Registrada. Bantam Books, 666 Fifth Avenue,
New York, New York 10103.

PRINTED IN THE UNITED STATES OF AMERICA

RAD   0 9 8 7 6 5 4 3 2

More Than
Meets
the Eye

JEANNE BETANCOURT

BANTAM BOOKS

NEW YORK · TORONTO · LONDON · SYDNEY · AUCKLAND